English class

I realized that this class must have been one of the bottom classes of the grade. Which was fine with me. It would be totally easy for me if this teacher didn't have any expectations at all.

"Well, you're gonna need to catch up." He got up and walked to his closet. He got a beat-up paperback copy of the book and handed it to me. "Where am I going to put you?"

We looked for an empty seat. I noticed Parole Girl from the guidance office sitting in the class. This was getting better by the minute.

"Okay, have a seat over there next to the waste product with the Walkman. The homely kid wearing the bandanna, the one desperately trying to look cool."

"I heard that," said a kid with long hair and a scowl.

"Congratulations, Glenn. You were supposed to hear it." Brody turned back to me. "Sorry to stick you in Loserville, but it's the only seat I have left."

"Your wife didn't think I was such a loser last night," the kid said. Several kids went "Ooooh!"

"Yeah, well. Look what she's used to. Even a demented child like you would seem like an improvement." Several kids laughed and clapped. Glenn gave Mr. Brody the finger. Mr. Brody smiled.

"Have a seat, Kirk. And welcome to the nuthouse."

OTHER SPEAK BOOKS

BLIND SIGHTED

peter moore

speak

An Imprint of Penguin Group (USA) Inc.

Thanks to Susan Kaufman for helping my book find a good home.

Many thanks to Jill Davis, editor extraordinaire, for her wisdom, insight, and humor, and for her persistence in guiding me to the best way to tell this story.

Most of all, I am enormously grateful to my wife Ellen, who has listened to my rambling for endless hours, who has read countless drafts, and whose support, encouragement, and love has kept me writing all these years.

SPEAK
Published by Penguin Group
Penguin Group (USA) Inc.
345 Hudson Street, New York, New York 10014, U.S.A.
Penguin Books Ltd, 80 Strand, London WC2R ORL, England
Penguin Books Australia Ltd, 250 Camberwell Road, Camberwell, Victoria 3124, Australia
Penguin Books Canada Ltd, 10 Alcorn Avenue, Toronto, Ontario, Canada M4V 3B2
Penguin Books (N.Z.) Ltd, 182-190 Wairau Road, Auckland 10, New Zealand

Published in the United States of America by Viking,
a division of Penguin Putnam Books for Young Readers, 2002
Published by Speak, an imprint of Penguin Group (USA) Inc., 2004

10 9 8 7 6 5 4 3 2 1

THE LIBRARY OF CONGRESS HAS CATALOGED THE VIKING EDITION AS FOLLOWS:
Moore, Peter.
Blind sighted / Peter Moore.
p. cm.
Summary: Kirk, a creative misfit who is in trouble at high school because he is bored with his classes, learns to deal with his alcoholic mother, new friends, and life with the help of a blind young woman who hires him to read to her.
ISBN 0-670-03543-2
[1. Coming of age—Fiction. 2. Interpersonal relations—Fiction. 3. High schools—Fiction. 4. Schools—Fiction. 5. Blind—Fiction. 6. People with disabilities—Fiction. 7. Alcoholism—Fiction.] I. Title.
PZ7.M787515 Bl 2002 [Fic]—dc21 2001056813

Set in Granjon

Speak ISBN 0-14-240126-9

Printed in the United States of America

for hedy and jake,
with all my love

BLIND SIGHTED

drone

Just kill me now. Drone, drone, drone. The person you
are trying to reach is disconnected. And he will
    stay that way, probably forever.
I can't stay
          The execution
Of this lesson is killing me.
The classrooms in this school
Like prison cells
Killing cells
    In my brain.
Class change bells
are soul-death knells.
"Poor conduct," they say.
I'm a conductor
in my electric chair
    Guilty of having no convictions
Convicted for crimes committed
As the Chairman of the Bored.

"Kirk, is there something funny?"

"Huh?" was my response, shining my powers of spoken language over all assembled in my class.

"You seem to find this discussion amusing," Mr. Mahoney said.

"Sorry," I said, turning the page in my notebook so he wouldn't see what I'd been writing.

"I hope you're as amused by your grade on the paper," he said as he began passing back our essays. That was Mr. Mahoney's idea of a snappy comeback. I don't know exactly how teachers are recruited, but based on my experience, the main qualification seemed to be a total lack of personality and humor.

Which actually made for a pretty good match with most of the students in the honors track.

"For the most part, these papers were quite good," he said in a monotone. "For the most part," he repeated as he dropped my paper in front of me. He tapped the front page three times with his long index finger.

Written on the cover page were the words, "This does not answer the assigned question and it makes no sense. 65." I looked up at him.

"It makes no sense?" I asked.

He grabbed it and opened it up. I thought it was pretty amazing that he did this in front of the class instead of maybe waiting until after.

"Just picking a point at the beginning. 'Wharton's literary devices are about as subtle as a stick in the eye, and not nearly as much fun. A much better use of metaphor can be found in *Slaughterhouse-Five*, by Kurt Vonnegut. He uses the bombing of Dresden to represent the death of compassion in the twentieth century. . . . ' And then from that point on, the entire paper is about *Slaughterhouse-Five*."

"It's a great book," I said.

"That may be, but what does it have to do with anything?"

"I think it's a much better use of metaphor."

"I'm not really interested in what you think. I'm interested in you answering the question I assigned."

Wow. Talk about hitting the nail on the head.

He shook his head and moved on, handing out more papers. I considered trying to explain my ideas, but what was the point. It was all just a waste of breath.

A little freshman girl knocked on the door as she came in.

"Ms. Vanucci wants to see Kirk Tobak. Is he in this class?"

"He certainly is," Mr. Mahoney said. The girl handed the note to Mr. Mahoney. He glanced at it and said to her, "Take him. Please."

I could feel her eyes on me as we walked down the hall. I could hear her breathing through her mouth past a deviated septum or something, a high-pitched huffing that made her sound like Darth Vader's baby sister.

"You're really in eleventh grade?" she asked me.

"Yeah."

"How come you're smaller than my brother and he's in seventh grade?"

"How come? Well, it's like this. I started out six foot six, and I'm working my way backward. I thought it'd be more interesting than doing the usual thing, growing up and getting bigger. Be an individual, go your own way," I said. She looked at me like I was speaking another language. Which is how a lot of people look at me.

"Okay. I can take it from here," I said when we got to the guidance office. She shrugged and turned on her heels. I pushed open the door and went in.

I rapped on Ms. Vanucci's open door and looked in. She had a kid in there already.

"Hi, Kirk. I'll be with you in a few minutes."

I nodded and had a seat in the waiting area. Across from me, a girl was slouched low in one of the fake leather chairs. She had wavy dark red hair and a big scowl on her face. Her fingers were all covered with cheap-looking silver rings, and she drummed her fingers on her gray fatigues. She slouched further and her shirt rode up a little. Her white belly was flat. She started twirling the silver bar in her belly button. A word popped into my mind: *parole*.

The kid walked out of the office and Ms. Vanucci smiled at me and waved me in.

"So," she began. "How are things going?"

"Fine. Same old thing."

"Mm. How are things in English?"

Ah. So that was it. "Okay. I had some pretty low grades, I guess."

"Well, as it happens, Mr. Mahoney spoke to me this morning. He showed me your grades. Why do you think they're so low?"

I shrugged.

"Do you pay attention in class?"

"Sometimes."

"Do you do homework?"

"Nope."

"Never?"

"In my life? I guess I have. Not too often."

"Do you study for tests?"

I laughed. I didn't mean to be obnoxious. I just couldn't help it.

"And Mr. Mahoney tells me that you sometimes do very well on the tests. He thinks it's when the material interests you."

"Which isn't too often."

"Which isn't too often, yes. Mr. Mahoney says you like to do your own thing, even though he's warned you about your grades. You still do what you want to do. I'll tell you, Kirk. It seems pretty clear that you're not willing to do what it takes to be in honors English."

If what it took to be in honors English was pretending to be interested or doing every boring, unimaginative homework assignment or smiling as Mr. Mahoney talked to me in that totally condescending critical way, then no, I wasn't willing to do what it took to stay. But I knew that would sound bad to say, so I just shrugged.

That's when I noticed she had a tiny little knickknack on her desk. It was a little chrome skier on a little chrome stand. The skier's feet had a pin coming out of the bottom of the skis and the pin stood on the tip of a tall, narrow post. The skier was made to stay perfectly balanced on the tiny post.

"So what do *you* think, Kirk? Where do you belong?"

"I honestly couldn't tell you."

Ms. Vanucci sighed and turned her chair to get my program card to take me out of honors English. Her chair banged into the desk. The skier wobbled back and forth, but he didn't fall. He would never fall. Unless he was knocked off.

After school, I walked through town to my job. This town is like a small town set from a fifties B-movie, where everything is perfectly normal, right until the invaders arrive. My guess is this town looks like a lot of towns all over the country, no better, no worse, unless you consider it worse just for being in New Jersey. I have to admit, it's just a guess that this is like other towns, because I haven't really been to too many other places, except for a couple of trips to New York and once to Philadelphia for a school trip. There was so much going on in those places that I wondered if everyone really knew where they were rushing to. A week after going to those cities, it seemed like I had dreamed it.

Anyway, the town where I live should really be called "NothingDoingVille." You have your bank, your stationery store, your small hardware store, your pizzeria with basically pretty bad pizza, your pet store with mostly empty cages except for some mice and two molting canaries, your liquor store, your florist, your tuxedo rental, your insurance agent, your bar with the neon SHAEFFER sign in the window, and that's about it. Like I said, there must be a billion places like this all over the country.

The thing about this place is that pretty much nobody

ever seems to leave. Sure, a bunch of the honors kids go to colleges other than the local community college, or they might somehow just pick up and leave. Once in a while someone takes off, or marries someone and moves away. But mostly people stick around, like flies on flypaper. They work in the hair and nails place or in a restaurant or a convenience store, or they work for the gas company or for the police department or fire department, or they pump gas, or get a job in a restaurant or store or in the mall out on Route 48. This isn't a Thornton Wilder kind of thing, though. It's not like people stay because it's so cozy and everyone loves each other. It's just that it seems like staying is what you do.

One other place we have is a library, which is where I worked after school.

"Afternoon, Kirk," said Margaret as I walked in. Margaret was the head librarian. She really loved the library and everything associated with it. I think she would have named her firstborn Dewey Decimal.

I grabbed the edge of the reshelving cart and started into the stacks. I guess I should make it clear that the term "stacks" barely managed to be plural. This wasn't exactly the Library of Congress. I wasn't going to wear out any sneakers walking from one end to the other to reshelve the books.

We had a pretty decent video collection, which was pretty convenient for me. Sure, I could have gone out on Route 48 to the Blockbuster, but why travel all that way, when I had movies right there where I worked? And why pay to rent them, when they were free at the library?

I was reshelving in biography and looking through a bio

of Zelda Fitzgerald that caught my eye. I liked reading about people who were considered wild or insane or different, or all three. I was reading about how Scott (it seems nobody called him Francis, or F.) kept having her committed to an insane asylum while he ran around having fun.

"Hi, Kirk. What do you have?" Janet, the other librarian, asked me.

"Just a bio of Zelda F. Total wacko."

Janet smiled and wiped her brow with the back of her hand. Janet was about twenty months pregnant, or at least that was how she looked. If you stood a VW bug on its back bumper and made it sweat nonstop, you'd have Janet. This was her first baby, and all the ladies in the library kept talking about it. They had given Janet a baby shower a week before, and I was invited, but I didn't feel comfortable going, being the only guy and all. I bought her a package of cool shaped baby bottles. I don't really know much about what you're supposed to get somebody in a situation like that. I sent them to the baby shower with Margaret.

"She was an interesting woman," Janet said. "I guess you've probably read a lot of Fitzgerald's work."

"Some, yeah. *Gatsby*, great, really great, a real American tragedy. Fitzgerald was cynical and romantic both in this great way that was so ahead of his time. *This Side of Paradise*, which kind of sucked, if you ask me, and *The Last Tycoon*, which I thought was pretty good, especially if you know about Thalberg, which is who it was based on, and the stories, which were good, at least the early ones, um, and I guess that's it." I stopped short, because she was getting The Look. The Look is how I notice people sometimes look at me when I get started talking. The Look is like this patient smile that basically says, *Boy am I sorry I asked; when will this guy just shut up and how do I get out of here?* When I do finally notice The Look, I usually try to cut it short and quit torturing people with my rambling. Like I said, when you get The Look enough, you learn to just shut up.

"He's a good writer, definitely," I said, really going out on a limb with that appraisal.

"He really is," Janet agreed. "You do know books."

I smiled. Actually, I do know books, being that reading has basically been my favorite activity since I was a little kid. I just took to it and always loved it. I'll read practically anything. There are always books to be read. They're reliable.

I got back to reshelving, trying to look like I was busy, even though Janet wasn't in any way like a slave-driver type. "So how's the critter?" I asked.

"Getting close. Another couple of weeks." She smiled and wiped her brow again. I didn't remember ever seeing someone sweat so much, not anyone who wasn't involved in a triathlon. In Mexico. In August.

"Kirk? Listen, there's something I've been meaning to ask you about. Do you like working here?"

I couldn't believe it. How do you get fired from a crappy library shelving job? "What? Sure. I mean, what did I do wrong? If this is about when I look at books, it's only when I'm done shelving, and I check to make sure that nothing else needs to be done."

"You're not in trouble," Janet said. She started fanning herself with the sheaf of paper in her hand. "It's just this night job I have that I won't be able to do once the baby comes, and I thought of you. Maybe you'd want it."

"Oh, well, thanks. But I can't take on another job right now." I made sure that I stopped there and didn't start yammering on. After all, we only had two weeks before the baby was supposed to be born.

"Well, it could be instead of working here."

"But I like working here. This is fine."

"It would be a great help to me if you would consider it."

"Well, what is it?"

"There's a woman outside of town. Three nights a week I go to her house and read to her."

"Why?"

"She's blind."

"Oh." I didn't really know what to say. I had no idea what to make of it.

"I've been doing it for almost two years. She's come to look forward to it and I hate to just leave her, but I won't be able to do it with the new baby and all. I know how you like to read and I thought this would be a nice match."

"Well, what about my job here at the library?"

"You could stop doing this and go to her in the afternoons instead. You'll be much better paid reading to her. And I think you'll find her interesting."

"What does she like to read? Hear, I mean."

"Almost anything. A lot of the things you seem to like. She's very open."

I didn't say anything. I just couldn't see myself sitting in this old lady's living room reading to her while she banged on the floor with her cane. To tell the truth, people with crippling kinds of things really freaked me out a little bit. I know how rotten that sounds, but I can't help it.

"Well, think about it, will you? I think it could be a good situation for everyone."

"Okay, well, I'll think about it, but I have to tell you. I'm not sure it'll work out. I have a lot of things to do after school, when I'm not here. And I'm not sure how I'd get there. And I'm not really used to reading out loud to someone."

I stopped talking when Janet keeled over and fainted.

I had never seen someone faint before. Only in the movies, where it's much more dramatic, as you'd guess. In life, she just crumpled into a heap. At first I thought she was playing some kind of joke, even though it wasn't really her personality to joke around, not like that. It took me a couple of seconds to realize what was really happening, and then I called for Margaret.

"Margaret? Um, help?"

"I'll be there in a minute."

"No, um, now? You really need to come here, right now."

She was there in, like, a few seconds and it only took a minute for Janet to come to, as they say in the old movies. It had just been the heat of the radiators, which they keep cranked pretty high in the library, making it sort of cozy and stuffy, like I imagine the inside of a kangaroo's pouch must be. So the heat and the pregnancy really knocked Janet for a loop, and she took a dive. Even though she was fine, it really freaked me out. I thought about it on my walk home. I felt weak and crappy, to be honest about it. I felt like I should have done something more, something heroic or something. I should have at least caught her, instead of letting her collapse into a pregnant heap. It was not a cool way to be.

n o t c o o l

We lived on what's usually called the wrong side of the tracks, except really most of the town was on the wrong side. We just lived on the more wrong side. The house was the house my mother grew up in. Her parents left it to her, and they died a few years before I was born. My mother and father lived there until he took off, which was when I was a little baby. So we stayed on.

The house was getting pretty rundown. The carpet was ancient and worn, the color of dried moss. The couch and chairs were at that comfortable stage after the really uncomfortable stage. In the breaking-down stage, there are inconvenient and awkward lumps and poky things, rebellious. Then the lumps and poky things settle a little, and then they eventually break down and the whole thing just becomes completely passive. I guess the life cycle of furniture is kind of like the life cycle of people.

The doors were also like old people, with wheezes and creaks that made each one of them cranky, but familiar. The doors led into rooms that were small and close, with windows that made horrible squealing sounds when you heaved them open, backed by screens with lots of patches. So my house was kind of worn out, but it was still hanging on. Stalwart, I guess, would be the word.

I found some chicken nuggets in the freezer and made some frozen fries with them to make a nice defrosted oily dinner. I sat on the couch and ate off the table while watching *The Godfather Part II*. Someone had returned it to the library right before I left, and I never got tired of watching it. Perfect acting, perfect writing, perfect direction, fantastic characters, the most intense conflicts, what more could you want?

Mom came home at her usual weekday time, ten-thirty. That was exactly how long it took her to count her tips, have a drink at the bar, and drive home.

"Oh, look how young he was," she said about Al Pacino as she pulled off her shoes. "He looks like a kid." She shook her head and rubbed her toes. "Is this part one or part two?"

"Two. You want me to rewind? I'll watch it again."

"Don't bother. I'm wiped out."

"Bad night?" I asked.

"No worse than usual."

"You ate at work?"

"Yeah."

"I think there are still some chicken nuggets left."

"That's okay. I just wanna have a drink and relax."

She took off her stockings and walked barefoot into the kitchen to get her drink.

"I'm going up," I called. I pushed eject on the VCR.

"See ya later. School okay?"

"Yup," I said from the stairs. There wasn't any point to telling her that I was being pulled from another class. It wasn't exactly an unusual event.

My room was small, mostly bed and an old desk. On the desk was my thirteen-inch TV, which was almost as old as I was. I had a VCR which someone had thrown away, left on a wet lawn out by the curb, and which I fixed myself. I didn't have posters or anything like that on my walls. I had put up some color plates from an art book the library was getting rid of a couple of years before. One was this Winslow Homer picture of this guy in a little rowboat, lost at sea. I also had this picture that Diane Arbus took which showed this messed-up looking family, two young parents and a kid that seems to have something really wrong with him. The picture both sickened me and attracted me at the same time. I guess you could say it was very compelling, like a car wreck.

I put the movie on, but I couldn't really concentrate on it. I was still bothered about what happened at the library, mainly what I did. Or didn't do, which is the point. I just let Janet drop to the floor. I watched her. I just stood there, calling for help, like some kind of a dimwit. Not exactly what Indiana Jones would have done. I'm no hero, not at all.

I watched Michael Corleone take control. Sure, he was evil, but man he was cool.

Not me. I'm so not cool.

I can't get a straight answer from my mom about which, but I was named after either Kirk Douglas or Captain Kirk. Either way, both of them were pretty cool.

She should have named me Luke. Luke is cool backward. The opposite of cool.

The next day, I had to go to the guidance office to get my admit slip to the new class. As I walked in, it occurred to me that whoever decided to name this area of school "guidance" had a pretty good sense of humor. Maybe there was just a misunderstanding: maybe it was called "guidance" because the adults working there had come for guidance and they all just got hired by accident.

"I have a little secret to tell you," Ms. Vanucci said. "I think you could have done the work in the honors class. I think you're pretty smart."

"I think you might be in the minority on that opinion," I said.

"Well, your test scores freshman year were quite high in some areas. But you didn't seem to get the work done then. And here you are, November of your junior year, and it looks like you're still not doing what you could do. You have the aptitude. You know what that means, right?"

Of course I knew what that meant. Aptitude: what I was capable of. Achievement was the next word, which was the crappy job I was doing, not meeting my aptitude. I'd been hearing this since middle school. They always wanted to get some kind of explanation, and I never had one to give them. All of this bothered them a lot more than it bothered me. I guess you could say that I had the *aptitude* to change and be a model student, it just wasn't something I cared enough to *achieve*.

"I think you could do this. But you don't seem to want to. You deliberately avoid doing the work you're supposed to do. You don't take anything seriously. You do things your way. I get the feeling you're trying to make some kind of point. Does that sound right?"

"You mean does it sound like the right thing to do or does it seem right, like correct?"

"This is what I'm talking about."

She watched me for a moment. I smiled. Then I realized that she probably thought my smile was meant to be sarcastic.

"Everything all right at home, Kirk?"

"Yup. Perfect."

"Your mother's okay?"

"She's great."

She nodded. And then she shook her head. "All right, then. I guess there isn't much else I can do if you don't want to talk."

That made me feel bad. "I'll talk. What do you want to talk about?"

"You know what I'd like to talk about. But you don't want to explain it to me, so let's just leave it at that. My door is open when you'd like to explain your behavior to me. Maybe you should think about it a bit. In the meantime, you'll be in Mr. Brody's class for English."

"Ms. Vanucci. I really don't know what they want me to

do. I don't really know why they're all so mad."

"You try people's patience, Kirk."

"Well. At least I try."

She looked at me.

"Get it? Okay, well. Um. I always say, if at first you don't succeed, try, try again."

"Good-bye, Kirk."

"That was pretty bad. Sorry. But Ms. Vanucci? Don't look at this as a failure. You're really okay at your job. It's not you. I'm impossible. Incorrigible. Unreasonable. Irredeemable."

"Good-bye, Kirk."

I smiled and waved, and then I hightailed it out of there.

That morning, I entered Mr. Brody's English class for the first time. I was one of the last ones to file in. The kids looked mostly like the worst the school has to offer, which, believe me, is pretty bad. Not that they were dangerous or serial killer types. They were the ones who had given up or been given up on. Every one of them was headed for a life bagging groceries or pumping gas or not working or having an endless series of babies or maybe going to jail for petty stuff. They knew it and the teachers knew it. Their parents knew it and I knew it. It was no secret, it was just a matter of time.

"You look lost."

I turned to the teacher, Mr. Brody. He was sitting on the desk. He was so plain-looking I didn't think I could have picked him out of a lineup one minute later. He had on a flannel shirt, like a lumberjack kind, no tie. Black jeans and boots. He was old, like maybe forty. His short ponytail only made him look older.

I handed him the admit slip.

"Good to meet you, Kirk. We're taking a test on *Of Mice and Men*, first three chapters. Have you read it?"

"Nope," I said.

Of course I'd read it. I might have still been in diapers when I read it the first time. I realized that this class must have been one of the bottom classes of the grade. Which was fine with me. It would be totally easy for me if this teacher didn't have any expectations at all.

"Well, you're gonna need to catch up." He got up and walked to his closet. He got a beat-up paperback copy of the book and handed it to me. "Where am I going to put you?"

We looked for an empty seat. I noticed Parole Girl from the guidance office sitting in the class. This was getting better by the minute.

"Okay, have a seat over there next to the waste product with the Walkman. The homely kid wearing the bandanna, the one desperately trying to look cool."

"I heard that," said a kid with long hair and a scowl.

"Congratulations, Glenn. You were supposed to hear it." Brody turned back to me. "Sorry to stick you in Loserville, but it's the only seat I have left."

"Your wife didn't think I was such a loser last night," the kid said. Several kids went "Ooooh!"

"Yeah, well. Look what she's used to. Even a demented child like you would seem like an improvement." Several kids laughed and clapped. Glenn gave Mr. Brody the finger. Mr. Brody smiled.

"Have a seat, Kirk. And welcome to the nuthouse."

Of course I was at the library after school. That's where I was every day after school. This may be the point where you might wonder why I never hung out with buddies or a girlfriend after school. The truth of the matter is that I really didn't have any friends to hang out with. I had had a best friend when I was little, Michael DePiero. We were pals in kindergarten and then after that, we did everything together. We played practically every day, detective, commando, and all kinds of adventure games. We watched the same shows and laughed at the same jokes. The one thing we knew for sure: we would be best friends forever.

But by third grade, Michael got more and more interested in Little League and soccer and basketball, and none of that interested me at all. Maybe part of it was because I just wasn't good at it, but anyway, chasing balls and throwing them at hoops and goals just seemed kind of pointless to me. It was no fun at all. He always wanted to do sports and I wanted to hang out and read. So we kind of drifted apart, and finally it got so we just kind of nodded when we passed each other in school.

By the time you're in fourth grade, pretty much all of the boys are into sports: if they're not playing them, they're watching them on TV or talking about them. And that made no sense to me either. I could never understand how people could get so worked up about a professional sports team. What did I care if the Yankees won or not? They weren't people I knew.

So that left me pretty much out of the loop. And the few

other kids who weren't into sports were into computers or video games or stuff like that, which also didn't interest me at all. So I stayed with my books.

There was a new guy named Walter working at the library. He was older and talked in a singsong voice, like he was on some kind of medication. Margaret told me that Janet had the baby. It seems that her water broke while she was driving home after the day she fainted. Margaret started going into details, telling me that her cervix had dilated to, like, nine centimeters, and her water broke while she was driving home. I actually turned around and bumped into a shelf, knocking two books off. I really didn't need to hear about Janet's dilating cervix, and frankly the idea of the front seat of her Accord being slick with amniotic fluid made my stomach lurch. Anyhow, Janet was fine and the baby was fine, and this Walter guy would be filling in for Janet for a while.

"Janet told me to ask you if you'd given any thought to what she asked you to do. She said you'd understand."

The blind woman. "Oh. I don't know. Are you going to be talking to her?"

"Janet wants to talk to you about it. Here's her number. She'll be home in a couple of days."

Great. Now Janet was going to pressure me into this horrible job, just because she couldn't do it. I was a sucker for guilt.

———

I was lying in my room when Mom called. "Did you eat anything?"

"I had a couple of hot dogs and the macaroni salad."

"Was that still good? I thought it was kind of old."

"It was okay."

"Did you smell it?"

"I ate it."

"But did you smell it first?"

"It was okay."

"What are you doing?"

"Reading the Elmore Leonard book you left downstairs."

"Oh no you don't. Don't get too into it, because I'm not done with it."

"I'll probably finish it in the next hour."

"Listen, if you're okay, I might not be home till later."

"I'm fine."

"Just Hal."

"Whatever."

"All right. See you tomorrow."

"Have a good time."

I knew, of course, that "later" meant she wouldn't be home that night. She did this sometimes. She sometimes hung around with Hal, the manager of the restaurant, a guy who liked to wear a black T-shirt and a black blazer. She called it "having a few laughs with Hal." I knew what it was about and she knew that I knew. We didn't really talk about it much. It never really bothered me. I understood that she needed company and stuff. I can understand that. I wasn't all that crazy about Hal. He called me "Champ" and

"Kid" and "Chief," which was basically pretty condescending and obnoxious. Whenever we were left alone for a few minutes, he didn't bother to talk to me much, unless he needed something from me. "Hey, Champ. Do me a big favor and pop into the kitchen and grab me that jar of peanuts, why doncha? And while you're up, how's about another beer. Thanks a million, Bucko. You're the best." Not exactly the most sincere guy I'd ever met.

Sometimes when he came over they would drink and laugh and talk about these crazy plans. They talked about running a bar/video-dating service, buying a racehorse, moving to Rio. Mom and Hal also used to take off on little trips together, like to Atlantic City for the weekend, or maybe Foxwoods for a few days in the week. I'd come home and find a note on the table and they'd be gone, with no warning. Not that it was any big deal, really, since I pretty much took care of myself anyway, but it still somehow seemed kind of wrong to leave a kid alone like that, especially when I was younger. Still, I guess, no harm done. It was just the way it was.

They were on and off over the years, and I got the feeling that a lot of times when they were off, it was because he was running around with someone else. Or sometimes she met someone else at the restaurant and had a few laughs with him. That was even worse than Hal, because you never can tell what kind of creep someone is underneath and I'd seen enough movies and read enough books to know what evil sometimes lurks. I could understand why she might do it, I guess, but it still got me edgy. I didn't usually sleep too well when she was with someone she'd just met, and I would call her at home in the morning from the pay phone outside the cafeteria. For some reason, that phone always smelled like grape bubble gum. But every time I'd call her, she'd just laugh and tell me that she was fine and that she could take care of herself and that I didn't have to worry about her and that she was the mother and I was the kid, after all. Now, whenever I smell grape bubble gum, it smells like relief.

I finished the Elmore Leonard book. I loved his dialogue. I wished I could talk tough like that. "I don't care if the broad is blind, I ain't readin' nothin' to nobody. I got my own problems, sister."

Yeah, right.

I wasn't tired, so I skimmed through *Of Mice and Men* and turned off the light.

"These tests were a disaster the likes of which have not been seen since the *Titanic* went down," Brody said, handing back the tests, facedown.

I looked over at the kid with the bandanna sitting next to me. He was what we called a burnout. Long hair, bored and out-of-it expression. He had on a flannel shirt with cut-off sleeves, open over a concert T-shirt. His jeans had huge holes at the knees, and he kept his long legs stretched out, his Doc Martens crossed at the ankle. He was writing in some odd letters on a sheet of paper. It looked kind of like:

A/Adim E Em F Eb7sus4 Em9+7

There were also a bunch of little tic-tac-toe looking boxes with dots in them. I thought about asking him what they were, but it was possible the guy was psychotic or something and was communicating with UFOs. I didn't want to take a chance of being stabbed or beamed up to the mother ship for anatomical experiments.

"This book is not beyond you guys. I'm not accepting these grades," he said. "Instead I'm going to let you do two short-answer questions as essays, due tomorrow." There were a bunch of groans. "No big deal, one page each. It doesn't have to be long, it just has to be brilliant."

"How long?" a girl asked.

"One page each."

He came toward me and scowled at the rock-and-roll kid next to me. "Very impressive, Glenn. Did you even *look* at the book?"

Bandanna Glenn didn't even glance at the test. He just swept it into his desk and continued writing his secret code.

"Did you get a chance to read the first chapters of the book?" Mr. Brody asked me.

I felt the eyes of the other kids watching me, sizing me up. "Uh, nope," I said.

"Not a very good start, is it?"

He shrugged and started across the room.

"Does watching the movie count?" I asked.

"Depends. Which one: Sinise and Malkovich or Mickey and the Wolfman?"

That was impressive. Mickey was Burgess Meredith, who played Mickey the coach in *Rocky*, and the Wolfman was Lon Chaney, Jr., who played the Wolfman in the

Wolfman movies. They were both in the first filmed version of *Of Mice and Men*, from 1939.

"Both," I said. "The new one is more subtle, but the one from thirty-nine has great melodrama."

"True. Thirty-nine was a big movie year." He looked at me. I could tell that a bunch of the kids were watching this, trying to figure out what we were talking about.

"*Gone with the Wind* and *The Wizard of Oz*."

"Not bad. Best Actor award?"

"Gable, of course."

"Wrong," he said. "Robert Donat, *Goodbye, Mr. Chips*."

I looked at him. This guy knew his movies.

"Maybe I can ask a simple question. That is, if you're done playing quiz show with the hobbit," the burnout said.

Brody looked at me for a moment. It almost looked like he winced, maybe figuring that the hobbit remark would crush me. He started to speak, but I turned toward the burnout myself.

"Hobbit. That's pretty good. You can read, I guess. Maybe more than the words on that paper they showed you, the paper they asked you to sign that said, 'You have the right to remain silent. . . .' Sound familiar to you?"

"Does the word 'dwarf tossing' sound familiar to you?" he asked. A bunch of "ooohs" erupted.

"That's two words, genius. Does the word 'inbred' sound familiar to you? And I thought this state had laws against cousins marrying!"

The kid turned and started to rise out of his seat. I grabbed the edge of my desk, wondering if I could pick it up high enough to hit him if I had to.

"All right," Mr. Brody said. "That's enough."

"Kid's a psycho midget, man," the burnout said. "I'm gonna kill the munchkin."

I looked at him, then at Mr. Brody. I was waiting to be thrown out.

"What are you waiting for, your standing ovation? Let's go," Mr. Brody said. "Sit down. We have work to do."

In the hallway after class I saw that Glenn guy from English standing with his burnout friends, who looked like refugees from Woodstock. I realized that I'd seen him around before, but the burnouts were sort of fringe people who kept a low profile. Kind of like me, too, but we were on different fringes.

Glenn saw me and squinted. I thought about turning around and going the other way, wondering if I was about to take a beating. He saw me, though, and I just couldn't go back. I kept walking toward him, forcing myself to keep eye contact. He ignored me when I passed.

"What the hell was that?" I heard one of his buddies say. "Did that kid just escape from kindergarten?"

"Nah," I heard Glenn say. "Nursery school."

I stopped. "Hey. At least I got through nursery school without needing a tutor."

There was a chorus of "ooohs" from his crowd. He came away from the wall and stood over me. My instinct was to take a step backward, but I forced myself not to, to look up at him.

"Listen, you little pissant. I'm gonna give you a break

since you're the runt of the litter, but next time you try to diss me, I'm gonna beat the living shit out of you. Get it?"

I'll admit that my heart was beating pretty hard. I was going to snap back, but his eyes were pretty fierce. This guy was a psycho, and he might actually break important parts of me. I figured caution was the better part of valor, or whatever that saying is, and decided to keep my mouth shut.

He kind of snorted, which I guessed was his idea of repartee, and he walked away. It looked like I had jumped out of the frying pan and into the toilet.

Mom didn't look too good when she got home. The thing about my mom is that she used to be really pretty, like almost cheerleader-pretty, except with a more interesting face. She still is pretty, but it's sort of faded. It's kind of like a picture of someone who's attractive, but the picture is a tiny bit out of focus. Their prettiness is blurred. I guess it got blurred for her by living in this town, dropping out of high school to have a kid. Working for sixteen years in a dark restaurant didn't help, and neither did getting loaded every night of the week. All of this might have the effect of wiping someone out.

So we watched TV, flipping around until she told me to stop on an old movie. She had a glass of vodka on her knee, the glass a bull's-eye in a wet ring on her terry-cloth robe. She had an ashtray on her belly.

On the TV, Cary Grant and Katharine Hepburn drove a leopard around in a car. She watched with a smile, but it wasn't like a smile bursting with happiness.

"You like this?" I asked.

"Yeah. I've seen it. It's good. But would you get me some ice, babe?"

I took her glass into the kitchen and got some ice for her. I know, it probably seems like I was helping her drink and all that and I was an accomplice or something like that. But the truth is that she was going to drink whether I got her some ice or not. It wasn't like anything I said or did was going to stop her.

So I got her the ice and gave her the glass. She poured another, held the glass up and looked at something, squinting and wrinkling her nose. Whatever she thought she saw seemed to have disappeared, and she took a good swallow.

"I coulda done this, you know," she said.

"What?"

"Acting. I did it in high school and I was pretty good."

"Really." This was not the first time we had this conversation. It was not even the hundredth time we'd had the conversation.

"Oh, I'm not saying I was another Kate Hepburn, but I was pretty good myself."

"Hm."

"You know who Tuesday Weld was?"

"Is. She's still alive."

"Is she?"

"I think. I'm pretty sure."

"Really? That's good."

Her thoughts got derailed a bit and she went back inside her head. I didn't much love this conversation. It made her sadder to talk about the old days, or what she used to do, and wasn't doing anymore. Sometimes after, late into the night, I'd hear her make moaning sounds in her sleep, or crying sounds. I have to say, it was really pretty depressing.

"You wanna go out for ice cream or something when this is over?" I asked.

"I'm not exactly up for driving."

"Oh." I was trying to think of some way to break her train of thought and keep her from going down the usual path.

"I'm just feeling like having another drink and maybe calling it a night." Which meant she was going to stay up late brooding. There wasn't too much I could do to get her out of it once she got on this track.

"Ya know . . ." she said.

"What?"

"Nothing."

"What?"

"Nothing."

There was no point in trying to convince her to speak. She was thinking about telling me something, but she wouldn't until she had decided she was completely ready.

We didn't speak anymore. We laughed a few times before the movie was over. I went up to bed. She stayed downstairs. I replayed the movie in my mind, shot by shot, until I fell asleep.

no guts

Unzip their heads and polish what's inside. Buff it up and make it shine. But read the Manufacturer's Warning: don't overbuff. Too much buff, megabuff, and you wear away what's there. Wearaway, whataway to wash and wear. Where, oh where has my little brain gone? Where were we? We were just going, move over, move down. Check out the new cave, and try the unzip. Let 'er rip, Oh Learned Ones, cause with this unzip, you end up with—you guessed it—zip.

Mr. Brody had told us to write for twenty minutes. The topic was open. I guess he felt that maybe somebody might write something if he left it loose. I looked around. It looked like a TV ad for apathy. I could hear the slogan: Nobody gives a damn about apathy. Many of them had their heads down. Some seemed to be drawing circles and shapes on their papers. The burnout next to me was doing his little tic-tac-toe boxes which I assumed were some form of communication with his home planet. I noticed the only person who was writing was Parole Girl. No doubt it was a marriage proposal to a serial killer in some federal pen in Kentucky.

I glanced over at Mr. Brody. He sat on the edge of his desk and gazed across the room, out the window. He had to be dreaming of a life where he could teach kids who had minds and personalities. That would be someplace very far from here.

He squeezed his eyes with his fingers and tilted his neck to the side, which made a cracking sound. He checked his watch and took a deep breath. He stood up and clapped his hands sharply.

"Okay, let's get back to the book." He said it in kind of a lively voice. The animation did not seem to be contagious. Judging from the reaction, everyone in the room might have been deaf.

"So we were talking about theme and we were talking about how many of the characters are lonely. Right?"

There was no response. I was starting to feel sorry for this guy. "Maybe I was the only one talking about it. Anyhow, in what ways are these people lonely?"

No response.

"Alice?"

Alice shrugged.

"David?"

"I dunno."

"Come on, guys. In what ways are the characters lonely? Eddie?"

"They all want sex and can't get it!" said Eddie, looking around for approval.

"We're talking about the book, not *you*, Ed," Brody

said. Eddie actually did a double take and a bunch of kids laughed. "Look. All of these people are very different, but they have one thing in common. What?"

No answer. The poor guy was getting nowhere. I couldn't stand it.

"Yes, Kirk. Save me."

"They're all lonely. They don't have anybody who understands them. The thing is, they all want to connect, but sometimes they just can't. The ranch guys aren't supposed to talk to the black guy, they're not supposed to talk to Curly's wife, because any kind of connection could mean trouble and they're all trying to avoid more trouble."

"Okay. Any comments on that?" Brody said.

"And another thing . . ." I said.

"Oh, my God. Is he still talking?" someone said. A few people laughed

"Another thing is that they all feel disappointed and they're trying to avoid more disappointment and one way to avoid it, which I guess is pretty common, is to stay by yourself and don't get attached to people."

The burnout Glenn let his head drop backward and pantomimed blowing his brains out.

"Well that does sound pretty grim," Brody said. "So they're just a bunch of lonely people." It felt kind of like it was just me talking to Brody and everyone else was in suspended animation or something.

"Well, I'd say most of them are really a bunch of losers," I added.

"Why do you say that?"

"Well, there are pretty much two kinds of people in the

story, right? The ones who are too afraid to have dreams, and the ones who have dreams which get blown away. Nobody wins. They all lose. They're losers."

"You're a loser. And you're a dwarf," said burnout Glenn.

I turned in my seat.

"That's true. I'm a loser. And I'm little. But lemme ask you this. What do you weigh, like two hundred?"

"About."

"See, now I'm about half that. Which means you're twice as big a loser as me."

There was a chorus of "ooohs" and some hollering. Brody had a small smile and turned back to his book. Parole Girl laughed.

"Burn!" she said. "He got you, Glenn." She laughed again.

But I realized from the way he glared at me that he didn't think it was too funny. I realized that I probably had crossed the line from obscurity to suicide.

I endured the rest of the day in all its boring dreariness until the class change between seventh and eighth period. I had to walk past the burnout crowd, including my new buddy. I kept my gaze kind of low and tried to keep walking at an even pace. Ah, right past him. No problem.

No such luck.

"Hey! Halt, hobbit! Don't move."

I stopped and turned. He pushed off the wall and

moved toward me. His pals watched us, smiling either from amusement or being high or both.

He poked a stiff finger in my chest. "For such a little guy, you have a pretty big mouth."

He yanked my notebook and it fell, scattering papers on the floor. Some girl said, "Glenn. He's just a little guy. Leave him alone." I think it was Parole Girl.

I looked at him. He looked down on me. "For such a big guy, you have a pretty small brain," I said.

No guts, no glory. I poked him hard in the chest.

He gave me a shove. It wasn't that hard, but I slipped on a piece of loose-leaf paper and fell. Without thinking, as I got to my feet, I swung a fist up into his gut.

He grabbed me by my shoulders and swung me around, spinning me into the lockers. It was loud, but it didn't really hurt.

I faced him and he faced me. I guess it was a standoff. I was thinking that a big club would come in handy. I knew that if he came after me, there'd be nothing left of me but a smear in the hallway. If I attacked, I'd better kill him with the first punch, which didn't seem too likely. We stared at each other and then, somehow, the moment passed.

It suddenly seemed ridiculous to fight. We both turned away from each other. I looked down at all my papers on the floor. It would be too humiliating to bend down and pick it all up. I didn't need any of it anyway. I left it and started down the hall.

"Hey. Your stuff," one of the burnouts called.

"He can keep it," I called back over my shoulder.

One Sunday when I was about nine, deeply involved in Tolkien's *The Two Towers*, Mom came into my room and told me we had to go visit Gram. Now this was a surprise, since, even though it was Mom's grandmother, we hadn't had much to do with her since she moved into her nursing home. It sounded like some harsh words had been said and they didn't talk much. Mom didn't usually make me have much to do with Gram, except send holiday cards. But suddenly, she said we had to go see her. When I asked why, I was told that she was getting sicker and she might not be around too much longer.

We stood outside the dayroom and I got kind of nervous. I could see in and, though there were lights on somehow the place looked kind of dim. It was faded, but that might have been the old folks in the room. "She doesn't look good, but you can't let her know that," Mom told me. "Just be nice and give her a kiss, you'll talk a few minutes, and then we can go."

We went in. I was hit by a smell like ammonia and freshly turned dirt. The place looked like it was a storage house for mummies. They were in wheelchairs and propped up in high-backed seats. Some of them played cards, but there didn't seem to be too much movement. Any time anyone moved, it looked like slow motion.

Mom moved me toward Gram. At about ten feet away, I stopped. Her hands looked like they were made of bones, veins, and wax paper. Her chin was working up and down, her mouth caved in, her lips shiny with saliva. She turned her head on a vulture-like neck and faced me. Her eyes were kind of sunken and the color of dishwater. She had a pretty wicked tremor, too. I caught a glimpse of a thick clear plastic tube curving out from under her thin bathrobe to someplace behind the wheelchair. There was a dark yellow liquid in the tube. The thing was, I didn't think I could go up to her and kiss her.

I knew it wasn't her fault that she was old and kind of falling apart. Still, I just had this totally nervous and disgusted and sort of freaked-out feeling. I knew I didn't have the guts to walk over to her, much less talk to her and give her a kiss. I wanted to bolt from the room.

Mom looked at me. Gram looked at me, though I wasn't even sure if she could see me, much less knew who I was. I knew right then that I couldn't handle old people, or infirmities. I just couldn't. But I also knew that I had to give this woman a kiss. I had to do it, because I couldn't just turn away from her. I had to do it because it was the right thing to do. I took a breath and moved forward.

I called Janet.

"So how's that baby doing, anyway?"

"Oh, he's great."

"It would be great to see him. And you, too, I mean. You're all recovered and everything?"

"Except for lack of sleep, I'm all recovered."

"Well, that's good. So, I was wondering about that job you mentioned. Reading to that lady?"

"Oh, good. I'm so glad you're interested."

"Well, I'm interested in being interested, you could say, at this point. I mean, you said she's kind of flexible about when I'd do it?"

"I think so. You work out those details with her. And I'm sure she'll pay better than the library pays you. I think this will be a wonderful match. Her name is Callie Curran. Let me give you her number."

"Oh, okay. But maybe you could call her first? Kind of set the stage, pave the way?"

"I'd be happy to. But you need to call her and set up the details."

"Thanks, Janet. I hope they're not mad at me at the library, though."

"They won't be."

I watched the first half of *The Shining*, but my mind wasn't on it. I tried to figure out what kind of books I'd be reading to an old lady. Did she like classics? Maybe she was into Jane Austen or Edith Wharton (who I'd tried, but couldn't really get into), or maybe Dickens (one of my favorites in ninth grade). I just hoped she wasn't going to make me read all trashy romance stuff. I'm pretty open about books, but there's some stuff I just can't take.

I waited until nine, to give Janet a chance to call first, and then I dialed the lady's number. It took six rings for her to answer. I imagined her pulling herself to her feet and shuffling across her living room, reaching her trembling hand to the phone.

"Hello," she said.

"Ms. Curran? Um, this is Kirk Tobak?"

"Yes, hi. Janet said you would be calling." Her voice was

kind of deep, but younger sounding than I had expected. She seemed very youthful.

"Oh, good. She called? Good. Yeah, Janet really is great, isn't she? A great person." Me, on the other hand, I'm a jerk.

"Yes, she is. She told you about the job?"

"Yes, she did. Well, a little. That you need someone to read to you. Not need, I didn't mean it like you need someone. I mean, that you're . . . that it's helpful to you to have someone who can read to you. That . . . it would be a help. For you." I thought of hanging up and using the phone to bludgeon myself to death.

"Is something the matter?"

Yes, I'm brain-dead. I'm an idiot. And now I can't speak.

"Is something wrong? Are you interested in the job?"

"No. Yes, I mean. No, nothing's wrong. I am interested. I'm not usually like this." Lie.

"Okay. Can you come by tomorrow and we'll see if this will work?"

"Sure. Absolutely."

She gave me the address and we agreed on six o'clock. After I hung up, I wondered if I would be able to do it.

I wondered about it late into the night and during classes the next day. I tuned out in English. My burned-out enemy wasn't there: sick or cutting. I couldn't even worry about him, because I was too busy worrying about the woman. I couldn't stop worrying that I'd totally freak if she took her black glasses off and she had milky-white blind eyes, staring off. I know it sounds awful, but it really got to me, the very thought of it. I was really afraid I couldn't handle it. I wondered if I could ask her to please keep her glasses on. But I knew that would be so horrible, so insulting. But wouldn't it be worse if she took them off and I just had this big reaction?

I went to the library after school, and I didn't say anything to Margaret. I had pretty serious doubts about whether I could work with the lady. I didn't want to get Margaret all worked up about me quitting the library if this new thing turned out to be nothing.

After work at the library, I walked two blocks into town and waited at the bus stop in front of the bank. It was a little ways out of town, where the lady lived, and I needed to get there faster than I could walk. I would have to come up with some transportation plan if she wanted me to work for her.

I had checked out *The Age of Innocence* by Edith Wharton, *Pride and Prejudice* by Jane Austen (just in case), and a book of poetry by Keats. I didn't know what she wanted, or if she would want me to read right away.

The bus ride was only about ten minutes. I got off outside of town, where the houses were a little nicer, the yards were a little bigger, the grass was a little greener. I walked up the side road, and came to a house that had the number she had told me on the phone.

I walked up the path and noticed that there was a light

on behind a thin white curtain that hung in a bay window. I was surprised that she would think to turn on lights. Why bother?

I took a couple of deep breaths and rang the bell. I hated being nervous. I felt like a creep. But still, I had trouble swallowing. After less than a minute, I heard a voice.

"Yes?"

"Hello. It's Kirk? Tobak?"

The door opened. I couldn't tell if it was her daughter or her granddaughter or maybe some helper or aide or maid or something. She looked at me and smiled.

"Hi. I'm here to see Ms. Curran."

"You found her. Hi, Kirk. And it's Callie. Come in."

I followed her inside. There was a little living room right next to where you came in and she walked across to a big chair and gestured to the couch.

"Have a seat," she said.

I sat down.

"Can I get you something to drink?" She was looking right at me.

"No, thanks. I'm totally fine."

She smiled, sat in the chair, and looked at me.

I couldn't figure it out. Obviously, she wasn't blind. I didn't know if Janet had been joking or tricking me, or if she meant blind as some kind of metaphor or something. The lamp I saw from outside was behind the chair she was sitting in, so she was kind of backlit, as they say in the movies. She was pretty small, and her hair was kind of blond, but with a little tinge of orange, I forget what that's called. I couldn't see her face too well from where I was sitting, with the light behind her. But I could see that she was looking right at me. She wasn't blind, not at all.

"So, did Janet tell you about the job?"

"Not really. Not very much. She said it was reading, but I don't know. Maybe I didn't really understand her."

"About what?"

"Oh. Well, nothing. I mean, maybe if you told me about the job, that might be the best thing."

"There isn't much to it. You read. I listen. We might talk about the books a little. I like that."

"Okay. Um. But . . ."

She tilted her head. "You seem as nervous here as you did on the phone. Is this too uncomfortable for you?"

"No, it's just confusing. I mean, I was maybe uncomfortable on the phone. But now, I just don't get it. You're not . . . you can see."

"Why do you say that?"

"Well, you're looking right at me."

She didn't say anything. I started to realize that I was the biggest dick in the world.

"I'm sorry. I can't tell you how sorry I am. I'm a jerk sometimes. It just looks like you're looking at me. I hope I didn't . . . you know. Act rude or something."

"Forget about it. I don't like the whole black glasses thing."

"Oh, me either. No, I'm just . . . Forget it. Sorry."

"Don't worry about it," she said.

I felt like I should crawl under a rock. I noticed then

that the place smelled really good. Kind of like cinnamon and roses and vanilla.

"Kirk? Forget it."

"Oh, the job, you mean? Oh, look. I don't blame you. You probably want someone who isn't such a . . . you probably want just a normal person. I'm sorry about what I said. Sorry I bothered you." I stood up.

"No, forget what you said. It's all right. Sit down, relax. Why don't you tell me what you like to read?"

"Me? Oh, just about anything. I like modern stuff, and some classic stuff, like Dickens is cool. Hemingway, Jay McInerney. I like Joyce Carol Oates."

"Me, too."

"Really? All kinds of stuff, really. I'm pretty open. I can read whatever you like. I like nonfiction, too. I read just about anything."

"Good," she said. "Not too many guys I went to high school with read as much as you do. That's great."

"Except, one thing, to tell the truth. And if it's your favorite, that's okay. I mean, really, if you want it, it's fine."

"What?"

"I'm not too big a fan of romance books."

"Me, either," she said. She smiled. She really had a nice smile. She wasn't exactly the crone I expected with a set of false choppers and big black glasses.

"So, I don't know. I guess you have to think about it."

"Well, I'll pay you twelve dollars an hour. We can start two or three times a week, two or three hours, however long you can handle. This time of day would be perfect. We'll see how it goes, if you want to give it a try."

"Wow, really? You don't need to hear me read or anything?"

"I'm guessing you know how."

"Pretty much, yeah. That's it? You mean I got the job?"

"Unless you have some deep dark secret, or you're a dangerous character or something you think I should know about, then sure, we'll try it."

"Wow. Well, great. That was easy."

"I'm a pretty good judge of character, I think. Why don't we start next week. Say Tuesday?"

"Great," I said. There was something I'd been wondering about and I had to ask. "I just have a question. I mean, they have books on tape and I guess Braille books. Why do you want to hire a person when you can have the book or tape whenever you want it?"

"Gee. A human being or a piece of magnetic tape. Pretty easy choice, wouldn't you say?"

broken spines

My notebook hit the desk with a loud smack. It was dropped there by Glenn, the papers sticking out from three sides, clearly just stuffed back into the binder.

"Here's your notebook," he said as he slouched into his seat. "You left it in the hall after your ass-beating."

"Thanks," I muttered. I didn't say anything else. I figured I probably wouldn't get lucky twice if I antagonized him again.

"Okay," Brody said. "Your essays are due tomorrow. I'm going to give you some time to work on them in class."

"How many pages does it have to be?" some girl asked.

"One page each. Two essays makes two pages." He actually did the math on the board: 1 page X 2 = 2 pages. I wanted to think he did it as a joke, but looking around me, it was possible that he did it to make sure they understood.

"Do we have to do both?" another sleepy-eyed girl asked.

"Do you have to? No," Brody said.

"We don't have to?"

"You don't have to do anything." Brody had a gentle smile on his face.

"Oh, cool. So what happens if I only do one of the essays?"

"You lose fifty points."

"But you said I didn't have to do both!"

"You don't have to do anything. If you're comfortable losing fifty points right off the bat, then only do one essay. It's your choice, Angela."

She made a face and put her head on her desk, watching her pen move around on her paper. I would have bet she was writing her own name over and over. I've seen girls do this, again and again and again, filling the page.

I glanced down at the back of my notebook. I had written "Choices. Make 'em. Live with 'em." I didn't remember writing it.

I glanced over next to me. Every day, this Glenn guy wrote those code letters and the tic-tac-toe boxes. He drew them, erased them, tilted his head back and closed his eyes, then wrote more. He did all of this during class. He totally ignored whatever else was going on. He was totally absorbed in his mysterious activities. I couldn't stand not knowing what they were.

"What is all that?" I asked quietly.

"What?"

"That. That stuff you write."

"Chords."

"What?"

"Guitar chords."

Aha. I should have guessed. "Are you any good?"

"Not bad. What, you play anything?"

"Just the radio."

"Okay, Kirk," Mr. Brody said. "Less lip-flapping and more ecrivere."

"What?" I asked. I hadn't understood the last part.

"Shut up and write," he said.

Glenn turned back to his chords, I turned back to my notebook. The assignment was kind of boring, so I looked at the kids around me, at the washouts, myself included, and I thought about this poem written by Allen Ginsberg, where he writes about his crowd, about how they were special, his feelings about the people around him. I wrote my own stuff for a little while as Mr. Brody wandered the room.

"What's this?" he said, picking up my notebook.

"Nothing, it's just some ramblings."

He looked at it for a moment and smiled, nodding. "Well. You mind if I read this out loud?"

"Yes."

"Tough. All right. Listen up, guys. This is a play on a poem that was written in the fifties. Ancient history to you. Listen:

> *"Hurl.*
> *I've seen the best of my generation clashing skulls on football fields and exhaling plumes of smoke and scattered hopes and dreams to rise up to nothing.*

I've seen their eyes glaze over to images of professional wrestling and video games.

I've seen girls turned into clones of models and pop stars, their minds a hash of hash.

Boys who hang and bang, churn and burn, crush and crash. They leave wreckage in their wake, but no waking for them.

It's all sleep, a walking talking sleep, a doze for days and days and days, dazed for years, left for life.

Call the EMT, for we are the empty."

Mr. Brody looked at me.

"Or not," I suggested.

There was a long silence in the room.

"That was pretty cheery," Glenn offered. "Maybe I'll go kill myself now."

"Want company?" I said.

"So this is actually pretty interesting," Mr. Brody said. "Maybe not the most uplifting thing I've ever read, but if you know the poem it's based on, you'll see what Kirk is doing. He's taking it, taking an approach, and making it his own. So here's what we'll do. Let's just bag the essays. Instead, each of you pick a poem from the poetry anthology and write a response in poem form. It can be a satire or a parody or any kind of response you like. You can start it now and finish for homework."

They were too dead to even groan and protest The ones who were still awake dragged open their notebooks.

Mr. Brody dropped my notebook on my desk and smiled.

"So I don't need to do the assignment, since I already did it."

"No, now you can do another one. Don't shortchange yourself."

Great. You show them you can do something decent and they ask for more.

I walked pretty much everywhere I needed to go. I was too old to ride a bike. And even if Mom didn't need the car all the time to get to work, I only had my learner's permit and I wasn't allowed to drive on my own until I turned seventeen. So I was used to walking. There was a cold light rain falling as I walked along Bergen Road, headed toward town.

A car slowed down next to me, going about my speed. Now I never knew much about cars, in fact I never really knew anything about cars, but I did know enough to tell that this car looked like it belonged in a wrecking yard. The paint job looked like it came out of a gallon can of Benjamin Moore flat black wall paint. The three hubcaps it had were mismatched, same as the tires. There was a sheet of plastic duct-taped to where one of the vent windows should have been. The back of the car said "Nova," but to me it looked more like it should have been called "Pile-o-Crap." The passenger window went down and I saw it was that Glenn guy.

"Where you goin'?" he asked.

"To the library."

"The library?"

"Yeah, it's this place where they have these things called books."

"Books? Yeah, I think I heard of them. The library's right near Nick's Pizza, right?"

"It's close."

"Well, I'm going there. Get in, I'll give you a ride."

"You're gonna give me a ride? Should I worry that I'm going to end up dismembered in the woods somewhere?"

"What day is it?"

"Friday."

"Well, I usually dismember on Tuesdays, so you're probably okay. Unless you talk too much."

I winced when I pulled open the door and it made moaning metal-on-metal sound. "I hope nobody sees me get into this heap. It'll wreck my reputation."

I usually stopped at Nick's before work, since I didn't eat lunch at school. So since this Glenn guy was going there anyway, it seemed pretty antisocial if that day I decided not to go. We had our slices at the counter. We ate without talking for a while, just like we didn't talk in the car on the way there. I don't know about him, but I really couldn't think of much to say.

"So, that was kind of a weird-ass thing you wrote," he said. "That poetry thing."

"Weird-ass. Isn't that what they used to call Walt Whitman?"

"Huh? I don't know. I mean that in kind of a good way. It had this feeling that I thought was cool."

I looked over at him. He didn't seem to be mocking me. "Thanks," I said.

"So you write a lot of stuff like that?"

"Some. It just kind of passes the time."

He nodded a few times and folded the pizza crust into his mouth. The gold hoop in his ear winked in the sun.

"So you play guitar," I said. "What, like in a band?"

"Nah. On my own."

"What kind of music?"

"Mainly blues-rock. Cray, Keb' Mo', Roy Buchanan. Roots, like Creedence. Who do you like?"

"Me? Oh, I like a good polka. Yodeling. That kind of stuff."

He looked at me as if he'd just gotten sprayed by a skunk.

"Kidding," I said.

"Well, you're weird enough that it could be true. What do you really like?"

"Well, I guess mostly older stuff. Buddy Holly. Roy Orbison."

"That's not much better. Anything from the last fifty years?"

"I like some earlier Bob Dylan. Does that count?"

"That counts. At least it's a step in the right direction."

"And Springsteen."

"Now you're talking."

"Well, I gotta get to work. Thanks for the ride."

"See ya."

"See ya."

I crossed the street to the library and looked back at the

pizza place. The window was all fogged up and the Glenn guy was just a faint, unformed shape.

Saturday night, I fell asleep watching a movie in my room. I woke up around one-thirty when I heard laughing from downstairs. I went down and found them sitting on the couch, Mom and Hal and Jack Daniel's. A quarter of the bottle was left.

"Hey," Hal said. "How's she goin', kid?"

"Hey, Hal."

"How's she hanging, Chief? Long and low, I hope."

I did my best to smile. I don't know how you answer something like that, especially in front of your mother. I tried to cover the awkward moment by rubbing my eyes.

"Oops. Didn't mean to wake you," Mom said. She looked at Hal, he looked at her, and they broke into a sputtering laugh. To get away from them, I went into the kitchen and poured myself a Pepsi.

"So are you going to remember all the little people on your way up?" Mom asked him.

"Well sure, Baby. Little people are important. Without *little* people, people like me wouldn't know we're *big* people!" She laughed at this like it was the funniest thing she'd ever heard. I didn't think it was so funny, mainly because I wasn't convinced that Hal totally meant it as a joke.

I felt trapped in the kitchen. If I didn't want to spend the rest of the night in there, I'd have to cross back through the living room. I could hear them murmuring something, talking in low tones, which could be the start of the romantic portion of the visit, which I could do without, thank you very much. I decided to make a break for it.

Even though I tried to keep my eyes down when I moved back through the living room, I could see that Hal's hand was on Mom's thigh, and he was whispering something in her ear. Her head was back and she laughed up at the ceiling, deep in her throat. I wanted to puke.

"Night, Champ," Hal called after me.

"Night, sweetie," Mom called.

"Night," I said, which I guess came out as more of a grunt right before I closed my door. I got into bed and put on the TV. I tried to force myself to sleep, to get away from my thoughts.

After school on Monday, as I walked out of the building, I passed by Glenn who was leaning on that horrible car. He mumbled the requisite "Hey" as I walked by.

"Howyadoing," I said. I started crossing the student parking lot when I heard him.

"Hey, hobbit. C'mere."

I walked to him.

"You doin' anything?" he asked. "You goin' to work or something?"

"I'm off today."

"Yeah? Well, anyways. I was planning to hang out at home until my girlfriend is done babysitting. I was gonna ask you if you felt like hangin' out."

"Hang out? And do what?"

"Well, I'm working something out on my guitar. I was gonna work on that. You could just kinda hang."

"Wow. Sounds pretty thrilling."

Now, I don't know who I was kidding. I couldn't remember the last time some kid had invited me over to hang around. I didn't work at the library on Mondays. And the truth is that I really didn't have anything better to do.

"Fine. Forget it," he said.

"No, you know what? Sure. I mean, I've been watching you write all those chords every single day. I might as well hear 'em."

He led the way to his car.

"Go ahead. Get in," Glenn said.

Glenn's house was a lot like mine, except less rundown. Someone was taking better care of it. Nobody was home when we got there: he told me his parents were working and his older sister was working at the roller rink. "You want a beer?" Glenn asked.

"Uh, no. I'm cool," I said, feeling like the most uncool person on the planet.

"Soda? What do you want?"

He took a beer and I had a soda. (He told me on the way over that he was almost eighteen. He got left back once.) He grabbed a bag of bargain-brand chips from the closet and led the way downstairs to the small basement. It smelled like mildew, which I guess was from the orange shag carpet on the floor. The furnace groaned.

I couldn't quite figure out how this had happened. The week before, this kid was one punch away from making me a homicide statistic. Now, I'm hanging out with him in his basement. Life could be so weird.

Glenn sat on a folding chair and picked up an electric guitar. He flicked on a four-foot-high amplifier and began playing a chugging, grinding rock song that I vaguely knew. He strummed and then picked out a lead. I had to admit to myself, he was pretty good. It really sounded like the song as I remembered it. He made a snapping sound with his mouth as he played, which I guessed was his way of keeping time. I was impressed.

"You know that song?" he asked, after finishing.

"Yeah. That was pretty good."

"I worked on it for a long time. I'm working on this other thing. It's not clean yet, doesn't sound that good."

"Go ahead."

"It might be annoying."

"Don't worry about it."

He started playing, some little parts he played over and over again.

I went across the basement and looked at the plastic bookshelves. They were loaded with cheap paperbacks with broken spines. There were books by Harold Robbins, Stephen King, Tom Clancy, a lot of detective novels. I looked at a few. The edges of the pages had what looked like grease marks. They smelled like coconut, and I figured the smears were from suntan lotion. I wondered who in Glenn's family read all these books.

After a while, he said, "Okay, I got that part. Listen to

this." He started playing. Now I don't know too much about music, but the song he was playing sounded pretty good to me. I guessed it was somewhere between blues and rock. It was kind of slow and had some real feeling to it. I guess soulful would be a good word.

His face was serious, concentrated, when he played. But it wasn't this totally fake, staged expression like I saw on the music videos when I flipped through the stations. This Glenn guy, he seemed to me like the real thing. Not that I knew anything about it, really, but that was how it seemed to me.

He finished playing and messed with some of the tuning things on his guitar. He didn't look at me when he said, "So that's what I've been working on. So, whatta ya think?"

"It was good. Do I know it?"

"I wrote it."

"Wow. That's really pretty impressive."

He shrugged. He continued playing with the tuning parts, not looking at me.

"So here's the thing," he said. "Here's why I invited you over."

"Uh-oh," I said.

"What?"

"Well, when someone says, 'Here's the real reason I called you here,' it's usually before the other guy gets strapped into a chair, or buried in the dirt floor and covered with cement or something. I've seen the TV movies."

"You're really pretty strange."

"Thanks."

He looked at me for a minute, then looked away and started messing with the amp. "So, anyways. I know music. I'm okay with that. But I can't write words for shit. And I kind of came to peace with that. But that thing you wrote in English? That was really pretty intense."

"That was just rambling gibberish."

"Well I've been thinking about it. Something about it stayed with me. Do you have more lyrics like that?"

"Lyrics?"

"Well, yeah. They're like lyrics."

"They're nonsense."

"Well, I liked it. And I was just thinking, maybe if you could write more stuff like that, I could use it with my music."

I looked at him. He glanced up to check out my reaction. "I'd give you credit and everything," he said.

"I don't know."

"Just think about it. If you want to, cool. If you don't want to, don't worry about it."

"Okay," I said.

"But I think it'd be pretty good. Anyway." He started playing again, something darker sounding, I figured more of a blues thing. I was listening. I got the feeling he was working hard at it, trying to show me that he was good. The whole thing was totally crazy. The stuff I wrote was just fooling around stuff. I was not a lyric writer, or any other kind of writer. Still, if he liked the stuff, I could sure churn it out. It might be kind of fun.

A while later, the doorbell rang.

"Downstairs!" Glenn shouted. It was a little startling.

He always spoke in a low tone, like he didn't have the energy for volume. Hearing him bellow like that was weird.

I heard a door open and someone walking around upstairs. Glenn cursed as he fought with some part of the music that he had been trying to work out for a while. There were footsteps coming downstairs.

"Hey." I heard a female voice. I looked toward the stairs.

Standing there was a female version of Glenn. She was pretty tall, with wavy hair parted in the middle, and she was wearing the female version of Glenn's burn-out clothes: an Indian print skirt and a flannel shirt, work boots. She had a lot of earrings in her ears and cheap-looking rings on all of her fingers, including her thumbs. All in all, I thought she was really pretty good-looking.

"Howzit goin'," Glenn said, working the same notes over, ending with him cursing again.

"What's up?" she said.

"That's Kirk. This is Donna."

"Hi," I said.

"How ya doin'," she said.

"Listen to this," Glenn said as Donna leaned her chest against his back and draped her arms around his neck. He started playing the song from the beginning. She swayed against his back. Then he hit the snagged part and cursed again.

"Sounded good till you bit it, there," she said.

"I can't get this part."

"You will," she said. She started to kiss him behind the ear.

"Well, I'm gonna go," I said. I got up kind of quickly.

"Hang out," Glenn said.

"No, I'll leave you guys. You can—"

"Hobbit, sit," Glenn said. "You can't go till we give you a ride anyways, and I wanna work this part out. Grab a book or something, take it easy, and we'll take you home in a little while."

"Fine. I'll wait. But in half an hour, I'm bustin' outta here," I said, doing a little Cagney. Donna looked at me.

"He's a total weirdo, but he's okay," Glenn said. She smiled. She had a nice smile.

"Who needs something to drink?" Donna asked, heading upstairs.

"I'm cool," Glenn said.

I settled back into the couch.

"Kirk?"

"I'm cool," I said. It sounded like a lie, but it felt pretty right.

Glenn and Donna drove me home. I sat in the back seat. My pants were sticking to something that I was afraid might be old gum. Donna grunted and moved around in the front seat.

"What, your back?" Glenn asked.

"Yeah. This weather kills." She leaned forward against the dash and cursed quietly.

"What's the matter?" I asked.

"You know what scoliosis is?"

"Yeah. It's like a curvature of the spine, right?"

"Right. Well, I had surgery for it and it still sometimes hurts like hell."

Glenn spun the wheel with his right hand. "They had to actually break her spine to fix it."

"Kind of," Donna said. I got the feeling she didn't really want to talk about it.

"She has a wicked scar, man. You should see it."

I didn't know a lot about scoliosis, but I'd heard back surgery was one of the worst kinds you could have. I wasn't sure if it was the scoliosis operation, but I had heard of some kind of back surgery where you have to be in a cast or a brace for years. I couldn't even imagine how that must have been for Donna.

I didn't tell Mom about hanging out with Glenn and Donna. It wasn't that I was keeping it from her. I just could tell that she had something on her mind. I could tell by the way she stirred the ice in her glass with her finger, just dunking the cubes and watching them pop up, like a little kid. She was putting the drinks back, one after another, and I didn't much feel like watching, so I went up a little early to call it a night.

I was still pretty amazed at hanging out with Glenn and Donna. I know it sounds pathetic and all, and it wasn't like we were best buddies all of a sudden, but the truth is I really didn't have any friends at all my age, and this was just such a weird thing to happen. Things like that didn't happen to me. It felt good.

But I thought about Donna's scoliosis and her pain. It's

one of those weird things where there's a whole part of someone's life that you don't even know existed. All the people who pass her in the halls don't know anything about that part of her. I pulled out the little notebook I kept next to my bed.

Stiletto pain may try to reign
My life, my mind, my soul
   "My kingdom numb, My will is done,
            now let me rest in peace."
Rest won't come and all my pains
To you are hidden
I am like Claude Rains:
You do not see any of me . . .
What color are tearstains?
My pain is all,
Invisible, nothing to see.

Sometimes it helped to write this kind of stuff. I couldn't really say what it meant, but I felt more peaceful after writing it out.

I woke up feeling like someone was watching me in the middle of the night. Which was exactly what was happening.

"What are you doing?" I croaked.

"So, here's an idea," Mom said. She was loaded.

"Now? We need an idea now?"

"Well, what about this. You ready?"

"So ready, I can't wait."

"You sure you're ready?"

"I'm so excited I can barely stay awake."

"So what if we just move."

"What? Move where?" I could see the ash from her cig‐ arette glowing, a spot of orange that moved with no pattern in front of me.

"Away. We could just move somewhere else."

"Like where?"

"Like somewhere better."

"Good night," I said.

"Seriously. How about California?"

"Good night," I said.

"Los Angeles? What do you say?"

"I say, good night."

"That's okay. You just think about it."

I thought about it for all of ten seconds before falling back asleep.

The next day, right before English class, Glenn asked me if I'd thought about what we talked about.

"A little," I lied. I actually kind of liked the idea. "But you only heard the one thing."

"You have any more?"

I passed my notebook to him. He read the thing I had written about pain the night before. I looked over at him at one point. He didn't look at me, but he must have known I was looking. I didn't know if he could tell that it was basically about Donna, or inspired by her, anyway. Still flipping through my notebook, he gave me a thumbs up.

"It's good," he said after class. Donna came over and

they kissed. She smiled at me. I sort of nodded. I felt a little awkward.

"The thing is," I said, "I don't know anything about music. Like the forms lyrics take. Refrains and all that."

"Don't worry about that. Just do it loose. The way you put words together is pretty funny. We can work it to help it go with the music. What do you think?"

"I think it sounds like Lennon and McCartney. Like Gilbert and Sullivan. Like Abbot and Costello. Like Smith and Wesson."

"That's what I'm talking about," he said. For the first time since I'd met him, I saw Glenn smile.

I was nervous going to my first night of reading for Callie Curran. It wasn't that I was nervous about her anymore, about her being blind, I mean. I just didn't really know how to read for her. I mean, obviously, I knew how to read. It's just that I wasn't used to reading out loud. Also, I felt like I didn't want to mess it up or disappoint her. At the library, all I had to do was shelve the books, not much to it. Here, though, there was more pressure to perform. Maybe not the same kind of pressure a person feels when working on the bomb squad or in hostage negotiations, but it still made me nervous.

When she opened the door, the smells of cooking blasted out and wrapped me like a warm blanket.

"Come on in, it's cold out there," she said. She held the door open and I moved past her.

"How're you doing?" I asked. "Boy, it smells great in here."

"I've been cooking all day. It's what I do. You can sit or follow me into the kitchen, I just have to finish something."

I followed her. She turned the light on as she entered.

She had an enormous stove with six electric burners. All of them had pots that were partly covered. More pots were hooked onto a rack that hung from chains attached to the ceiling.

Even though there was a lot of stuff going on, it was the most neatly arranged kitchen I had ever seen. Everything was lined up perfectly.

She had a pot in the sink with a rack in it that was lined with some gauzy cloth. She took the cover off a pot and hung the cover from one of a bunch of hooks that were mounted on the bottom edge of the cabinet above the stove. She poured the stuff into the gauzy cloth and then lifted the edges of the cloth, brought them together, and squeezed it. The pot was filled with a steaming, pale green creamy soup. My mouth watered.

"Wow. That smells good. What is it?"

"Potato leek. Grab a mug from the last cabinet."

"No, no. I wasn't trying to ask you to feed me. I just—"

"Oh, please. Don't ever try to refuse my food. Just get the cup."

She pulled open a drawer and reached in. She took out a ladle, without looking. Of course. She reached out in my direction and I handed her the cup. She filled it and handed it back to me.

I had never, ever had soup like that in my whole life. I'll admit, most of my experience with soup came from the can, but I've been in restaurants where the soup was supposed to be good, and it was, but nothing came close to this.

"Good?" she asked.

"Oh my God." It was all I could say.

She ladled the soup into a bunch of plastic containers that she had lined up on the counter. She reached above the sink where there was a paper roll of printed gold stickers. She peeled off a bunch of them and stuck them on the containers. I saw the stickers said "Callie's Cooking" in kind of fancy print.

"Whenever you're done, we can get started," she said.

"I'm finished," I said. "It was great. Really great. Thanks."

She held out her hand and I handed her the mug. It was the first time I got to see her face in the light.

I could see she probably wasn't older than like thirty or so. There was a little bump at the bridge of her nose, which looked like maybe it had got broken or something. In the light, I could see a network of tiny white scars that sort of radiated out from her eyes, over her forehead and the tops of her cheeks. It looked a little like a thick, wide-spaced spiderweb was draped on her face. I couldn't imagine what could cause scarring like that, but I guessed it had something to do with her being blind. Whatever happened, it must have been pretty horrible. I shivered.

"Let me get you a drink before we get started."

"Oh, I'm okay. Really."

"You're going to get dry if you read for a long time. Iced tea okay?"

It was the best iced tea. It was kind of minty, but also lemony and a little spicy. I asked her what was in it.

"Aha. Sorry. Top secret." She smiled and turned back to the stove, where she brushed her fingers over the dials on the stove, checking to see that they were all in the off position.

We moved to the living room. When she walked around the house, she didn't touch any of the walls or anything to guide herself. She just walked, stopped, and sat. She knew exactly where everything was. I remembered a joke that made the rounds in middle school which was: How did Helen Keller's parents punish her? They moved the furniture. I remembered thinking it was funny in seventh grade. I didn't find it so funny anymore.

She sat in her chair. I sat in a matching chair, facing her. We had agreed on *Catch-22*, which was great for me, since I had always wanted to read it.

"I don't know how you want me to read this. I mean, should I do different voices and stuff?"

"Whatever you want. If you're good at voices, go for it."

I was about to start, when I heard bells and chimes going off from a bunch of rooms in the house. There was this great big grandfather clock right behind me that scared the crap out of me at first. It had a deep gong sound that I could feel in my breastbone when it rang.

"Wow. You sure have a lot of clocks going."

"I like them better than the kind that announces the time with a mechanical voice. That's kind of creepy to me. I only use them when I have to."

I hadn't thought about it, but she couldn't just look at

the clock to see what time it was. But I liked her choice. I hadn't heard a talking clock before, but I guessed it probably would be kind of weird.

I started reading, but I was going too fast. I'm kind of a fast reader and I had to get used to slowing down. She told me to read at the same speed I would talk to someone. I settled into the couch and read.

The clocks chimed on every half hour. I lost count. We both got into the reading. I did voices, and she laughed when something was funny. She had a great laugh. It came from deep inside her.

"Hey, it's pretty late," she said. "I was only supposed to keep you here until eight."

"Oh, it's okay."

"Well, let's call it a night anyway. We'll pick up where we left off."

"So this is okay? You want me to come back?"

"Of course. You're a great reader. Next time, we can talk about the book a little, too. This should work out fine, if you're interested."

"Definitely."

" Tomorrow and Thursday are no good for me. Friday? Oh, you probably have plans?"

"Are you kidding? You don't know me well yet. Believe me, I don't have plans."

"Okay. Fine."

I pulled on my coat and went to the door. She followed and opened the door. "I'll see you Friday, then." I winced. I had to watch what I said. "Sorry, I mean—"

"See you Friday," she said.

I took the bus back most of the way and walked the rest. It was starting to get cold, but I didn't mind.

I was in kind of a loud mood when I got home. Mom was still at work, and I did what I often did when I was home alone and in a loud, good mood. It's kind of embarrassing to say, but I talk out loud, in different voices. I know that sounds like I should be committed to the local nuthouse, but it isn't like that. It's not like I think I'm talking to anyone. Obviously, I know I'm alone. I just kind of narrate what's going on, or kind of say what I'm feeling or thinking. I do it in cartoon voices, or maybe crazy foreign accents. I know it's kind of weird and a little immature, but it's entertaining for me, and it can fill an empty house with sound.

"Oh, baby. The kid is back!" I bellowed in a nasal, baseball announcer's voice. "He's back and better than ever. Yessir, the kid is home, but he needs some fuel."

"Roger that, Mission Control, we need to refuel in a big way," I said in a Southern drawl. "If we don't load up real soon, we may have an afterburner failure." I searched through the refrigerator and came up with a whole lot of nothing. I checked the cupboard.

"And he finds the all-American standby." This time a radio announcer's voice, the voice of advertising. "Yes, folks, you guessed it. He has found a nutritious and enjoyable box of mac and cheese. That's right, folks. Once again, mac and cheese saves the day."

I was in a good mood all night. I was smiling as I got into bed.

When I was about ten, I used to collect these little plastic soldiers. They were less than an inch high, and incredibly detailed. There were soldiers from all forces in WWII, and WWI, but there were also cowboys and ancient Romans and knights.

Other kids were out playing baseball and soccer. I'd get books about historical times from the library, research stuff, and spend hours building elaborate scenes, re-creating battles, moving the little guys all over. I had favorites, and for some reason, I liked having duplicates of these guys. So I would go to this hobby shop/toy store in town that carried them. I'd buy a little box, which usually had about thirty-six guys in it. But sometimes I was really buying the whole box for just one or two of the guys. That left over thirty perfectly good ones that I really didn't need.

I didn't throw them out. After I twisted each guy off the plastic spine that they were attached to, I'd pocket the few I needed. Then as I walked home, I'd leave the rest of the guys in little piles of three or four, leave them on the curb. Some kid would find them and it would be like a little gift from a stranger.

Sometimes good things just happened to you. The carnival would come to town. You'd see a movie that turned out to be so great. Sometimes you'd find things. You'd be walking along, and there was a dollar, just lying there. There's a penknife. There's a pile of cool little ancient Roman soldiers with detachable shields. But my belief was that the right thing to do, to keep the balance, was to make sure you did good things, too. Maybe leave the dollar for someone else to pick up. Maybe leave things for other people.

What goes around, comes around, I figured, though I didn't put it in those words. Leave something today. Maybe something good will happen later.

It had been a while, but suddenly, good things seemed to be happening for me.

half-baked

Gym class was forty minutes scheduled entirely for my humiliation. Being small was one thing, but being uncoordinated, weak, and lacking any athletic ability whatsoever was something else. I wasn't last to be picked on teams. I wasn't picked at all. I was a leftover who went to whatever team hadn't already picked the last breathing, eligible kid. It wasn't that it was bad to get me on the team. It was accepted by everyone that I more or less wasn't even there.

To put it in math terms, I wasn't a positive integer, and I wasn't a negative integer. I was the integer with no value. I was zero.

In November, we still went outside for gym. Whether this was sadism on the part of the gym teachers or a way to postpone the endless months of humidity and sneaker squeaks in the gym, I have no idea. They sent us packing up the hill, which in November was usually either muddy or frozen.

This November was different for me. Since I had to switch English class, they flipped my schedule and gave me a different period for gym. It was the same period that Glenn had gym, and once in a while, we were doing the same activities.

I didn't want to embarrass him by tagging along or glomming onto him, so I kept my distance. There were about ten guys between us as we trudged up the hill. It made me think of WWII movies, of troops heading for the Battle of the Bulge.

Glenn was one of the captains for the day, picking teams for touch football. I lingered on the fringes of the kids being picked. I always saw this process as humiliating for the kids begging to be picked. I knew I would barely be a part of the game, which was fine with me. But these poor slobs stood there watching the ad hoc captains pick, waiting, eyes like a puppy's in the pet store, silently begging "Pick me! Pick me!"

To my surprise, Glenn pointed at me when there were still plenty of people left. "Come on," he said.

"Me?"

"You."

We huffed into our cupped hands, stomped our feet between plays. Glenn played well. He was a tall and rangy kid. It's not like he was a jock, but he just had natural ease. He didn't take it especially seriously. He didn't have to. It just came to him. There was nothing to prove.

Glenn noticed my lingering around near the sidelines. "You playing or what?" he called.

"I'm in the game, coach. I'm in the game."

"Well, do something, then. Don't just hang around the edges."

"I can't do anything."

"At least get in the huddle."

I trotted over. It was kind of cool to be in the huddle, even though I didn't really understand what they were talking about. I clapped with them at the end of the huddle, my freezing hands buzzing like bee stings. As soon as the play started, I ran close to the sidelines to get out of the way.

Glenn saw me, saw I was open, and cocked his hand back to throw to me. I shook my head. The ball would either hit me in the face, or bounce off my chest, or I'd miss it by a mile. I didn't want it. Glenn could tell and he spared me.

After a few more plays, I got used to being in the huddle, and I was starting to like the feeling. When we were defense, I ran like hell after the guy with the ball. I could never in a million years catch anyone, but I gave it a shot.

We got a reversal or an interception or whatever it's called, and there was time for one more play. Glenn was calling out some complicated thing, a "Hail Mary Flea-flicker" or something like that.

"Well, we got the flea!" someone said. A bunch of laughs. Har, har.

"Listen up, we got a couple of seconds," Glenn said.

"Give me the ball," I said.

"What?"

"Give it to me. Don't pass it, 'cause I won't catch it. But if you hand it off to me, I'll run it through."

There were nine pairs of eyes staring at me.

"I'm serious. Look. They'll never ever expect me to get the ball. They won't even be looking at me. Fake to someone else, slip it to me, and I'll take it in. I'm your secret weapon."

Glenn looked at me, then at the other kids.

"Hut, hut, hike!" Glenn shouted.

We suddenly had a whole bunch of guys in motion. Glenn faked a handoff to Frank La Rocca, the big guy in English who called me a dwarf loser. Every kid on the other team either went after La Rocca or watched him run.

Glenn handed the ball to me and I trotted along toward their end zone, icy grass crunching under my sneakers. I was three-quarters of the way there when La Rocca went down under four guys. He held open his arms to show he didn't have the ball. Everyone started looking around.

Then they saw me.

I broke into a run.

It was cake.

I scored.

I went to hang out with Glenn and Donna some more. One time I bought a couple of boxes of doughnuts. I just wanted to give them something, even if it was just doughnuts. I guess I felt glad that they were being my friends. Of course, I didn't say that or anything, but it was how I felt. You might say it was that I felt grateful.

I worked up a few more ramblings, or riffs, as Glenn called them. They were clever enough, I guess, but I wouldn't exactly have said that T. S. Eliot was likely spending his afterlife worried that he was going to be eclipsed by young Kirk M. Tobak. As much as Glenn was impressed by these riffs, I wasn't. They weren't coming so easily anymore. I guessed that might have been because now I knew that someone else would be reading them, doing something with them. They suddenly had a purpose beyond being for my own entertainment, and I wanted them to be good.

> The other side of the mirror
> ~~Pass me one of those beers~~
> ~~It feels really weird~~
> Am I still in second tier or
> Waiting in the wings?
> These things I think
> there, for I am so late
> Isolate
>   ~~Isolater~~
>   ~~Isolatest~~
> ~~News from the front! I'm back!~~
> How I'm isolated, insulated.
> Now I'm elevated, consolated.

"That's pretty cool," Donna said.

"I don't like it. The end is no good."

"Why not?" Glenn asked, looking it over.

"There's no such word as 'consolated,'" I said.

"There's not? Doesn't it mean to make someone feel better?" Donna asked.

"It's really 'consoled.' I made up 'consolated' and you can't do that."

"Why not?" Glenn asked.

"You can't just make up words," I said.

"Says who, the Vocabulary Police?" he said. "I like it. Let's keep it."

He played some chord progression and then pushed hard on a last note and sang, "Con-so-LATE-ed . . . " He switched some of the chords and tried it again. "You think that would go with the one that starts . . ." Glenn asked and then he began playing a thrumming song I had heard him working on.

"Maybe. You have to write more of it," she told me.

"It could have an 'I Am the Walrus' rhythm," Glenn said.

This is how we spent our afternoons that week.

The problem was that it was becoming a hassle having to go to the library for work and then going over to Glenn's after. It made for a late night. Not that it got in the way of doing homework, since I didn't really ever do it anyway. The idea that I even had a social life was pretty funny to me, but there it was. I had to figure something out.

I was eating and reading some crazy stuff by William Burroughs when Mom came in from work. "Want some nachos?" I asked.

"That's your dinner?"

"Perfectly balanced. I got the chips group, the salsa group, the fat group. All that's missing is the chocolate group."

"I'll pass, thanks," she said as she sat down at the ancient kitchen table. It was one of those linoleum jobs with the chrome edge around it.

Mom sat in one of the chairs, rubbing her feet.

"Did you eat at work?" I asked.

"I had a little something."

"So guess what? I got this new job."

"What happened to the library job?"

"Well, right now I still have it, but this is really pretty interesting. I'm reading books to this lady who's blind."

"What? Who is this person?"

"Janet at the library, the one who had the baby? She used to do it and now I'm doing it. This woman seems nice. She's just out of town, on Weaver. And she pays like twice what I make at the library."

"Why doesn't she read Braille? Or why not use those books on tape?"

"I think she likes the company."

Mom frowned a little. "All right. If you think it's good, then fine, I suppose."

I didn't say much for a while. I just ate. She didn't seem like she was in much of a talking mood. She hadn't been for about a week. But I could see something was on her mind. I could tell by the way she drank and the way she picked at her fingers, tearing tiny little strips of flesh from around her fingernails. It was probably worse to watch than to do. To be honest, I had the same habit myself when I got edgy. My fingers could be ragged for weeks if I was nervous about something.

She poured a drink and sat back at the table.

"Did you think about what we talked about?" she asked.

"What's that?"

"About moving."

"I thought you were kidding."

"Not at all. I'm serious. Why don't we just get the hell out of here?"

I looked at her. She was serious as a heart attack, as they say.

"I don't want to move."

"This is a dead-end place. How many times did you say that to me?" she asked.

"But it's different now."

"It's exactly the same as it's always been. That's the point. It's *never* different."

"Well, it's different for me, now."

She was looking at me, and I was stuck between being mad and feeling bad for her. She had a horrible look on her face. It was the look I imagined people had when their doctors gave them really bad news.

"I mean, what were you thinking about? California? Why there?" I asked.

"It's warm, all the time. Sunshine. Beautiful houses."

"Somehow, I don't think we'd end up living in Beverly Hills or Malibu."

"No, but we could drive through."

"Wow. Sounds great. I mean, what about money?"

"That wouldn't be a problem."

I looked at her. Something was up. "What's this really all about?"

She looked at me and put on a smile, which I didn't trust. "Well, there are some big things happening. Remember when Hal was over the other night?"

"Go on," I said.

"You remember?"

"I remember. Go on."

"Well, you remember that we were both in a pretty good mood. And the reason for that is that we were talking about these big things."

"What's this all about?" She was obviously stalling and I didn't like the sound of it.

She put her hands around the salt shaker. "Well, Hal heard from this guy he knows who has a cousin who lives in L.A. There's a restaurant that someone's trying to sell. Hal would buy it, and I'd help him run it. We would move to California."

Now she had gone off the deep end. "You and me and Hal living together in a house in L.A. Is that what you're saying? I mean, are you telling me you're gonna marry him?"

She took a breath. "Well, we didn't decide anything definitely. But we want to make this commitment."

"This commitment? What does that mean, commitment?"

"It means what it means. Moving together. Working together. Probably living together. We would be a family."

"Hal?"

"Hey, we've been together a long time."

"Together? How were you together, other than the obvious, I mean? In all this time, he never made a commitment, as you call it. The only thing Hal is committed to is cheating whenever he feels like it."

"Okay, you'd better watch it, now."

"Mom, the guy is a player. Didn't you tell me you couldn't trust him?"

"That was a long time ago and it's different now."

"It's not."

"Maybe you're letting the fact that you're not totally crazy about him, which, by the way, I don't understand, since I think he's made plenty of efforts to get close to you—"

"What?" I shouted. "Are you kidding me?"

"He has, and anyway, you may not like him so much, but I think once we're together in a new, decent place, it could all work out."

"I have a life here now."

"Well I don't."

She slapped her hand on the table and some of her drink escaped from the glass. I looked at the ice cubes and remembered a book I once read about subliminal advertising. It claimed that in one magazine ad, if you looked at the ice cubes carefully, you could see that pictures of death's head skulls were painted onto the side of the cubes. I wondered if I would find skulls in my Mom's ice cubes.

I got up and washed my bowl. "I'll be in my room."

"I can't believe you're not completely excited about this."

"I'm not. Not at all. I hate it. I'm not going."

I started out of the kitchen.

She wasn't the best at arguments, even when she was

sober. Or when she was right. And she was neither, this time.

"Once you think about it, you'll change your mind. You'll see."

"Look, I don't know what you want me to say. Actually, I do know what you want me to say, but I'm not saying it. The whole idea seems horrible to me in every way," I said.

"I think it's a great idea. And I think we should go."

"I don't. No offense, but I think it's a really, really bad idea. Sorry." I left the room.

"Who's the parent around here, anyway," she called to me.

"I dunno. It's hard to say," I called back.

I had trouble sleeping that night. I didn't like fighting with her. It was usually a pretty even fight. She was older, but I was always a pretty good debater. And it was a tie in the stubbornness category.

At three, I peeped out my bedroom door. The light was on in the living room. She could have fallen asleep, or she might have been up, brooding and drinking. Either way, I hoped she would just get looped enough to forget her whole crazy idea.

She was fast asleep on the couch when I left for school.

In English class, Glenn asked me if I cared if he needed to repeat some of the lines in the riffs so they fit in better with the music. I told him he could do whatever he wanted.

"Let's back up a bit," Mr. Brody said. "Think back to the beginning. George seems to be the smart one, and Lennie is not too bright. Correct?"

No response, as usual.

"Correct?" he said louder.

There was a halfhearted murmur of agreement.

"Fine. But then we see that Lennie is sharp enough to play George, to manipulate him. He may not be exactly what he seemed to be. What do we call that?"

"A smart retard," a thickneck football player named Derek Fortuna said.

"Stop talking about yourself, Derek," Parole Girl said. This got a pretty good laugh. "And besides, you aren't smart." I didn't know she had a sense of humor.

"Okay, my question is what is this called in literature? It's called 'appearance versus reality.' Which is something you're going to need to understand when you write the essay I'm going to assign in about ten minutes." While the room filled with the usual moans of protest, he wrote APPEARANCE v. REALITY in huge letters on the board. "You're gonna see it all the time. It means that things are not always what they appear to be."

After school, I went to the library and told Margaret that I was going to have to stop working there. I explained that the hours weren't working for me anymore and that I had found a job I liked that paid twice as much as the library. She was nice and said she didn't need me to give notice. There was another kid who was waiting to have my job. She gave me a hug, which was the only sign I ever saw that she had any emotions at all.

At Glenn's, I didn't feel like talking too much. Glenn didn't complain. He had plenty of stuff to work on. Donna worked on her nails, trying to paint tiny pandas on them. They looked more like tiny crossword puzzles.

I was still bothered by the argument with Mom. I couldn't believe she wanted to pick up our lives to run off and go with that guy, that total jerk-off. Commitment my ass. I was fired up and dying to write down something, to get it out.

> Commitment. Four-letter word wearing a disguise.
> Discussing, disgusting discussion.
>   Committed means put in the loony bin.
>   Committed is the action of suicide.
> Come, Omit commit.
> I'm out.

When I got home, I had some frozen fish sticks and Tater Tots. I watched an old Steve Martin movie in my room, then turned off my light, but I couldn't fall asleep. I heard Mom come in around one. She pushed open my bedroom door. The light from the hallway framed her silhouette. She was a dark shape.

"You know, Hal and I are really talking about this California thing."

"Right. Like you talked about opening bars, and buying horses, and being talent agents for beauty contestants. Talking like that?"

"Really. This could actually work."

"Right."

"I'm serious."

"Okay. Whatever."

She didn't say anything for a few seconds.

"You're very stubborn."

"Wonder where I get it."

She stood there for a moment. I turned away from her. I could hear her breathing from across the room. I stared at the wall. As she closed my door, the shaft of light on my wall got smaller and smaller until there was total darkness.

Callie gave me a glass of her great iced tea and we got right to the reading. We went for an hour and a half, which was marked by the tolling of her clocks, and then we decided to talk about the book for a while.

We went into the kitchen, which was the source of the spicy seafood smell that had been distracting me from the reading.

"What are you cooking? It smells great."

"Cazuela. It's a Spanish seafood stew. Have a seat."

"You must think I come here begging for food. I didn't mean it that way."

"I'm not going to go through this with you every time. Sit."

She brought over two bowls of steaming stew. It smelled great, garlic and onion and pepper and fish and . . .

"Um . . ."

"What's the matter?"

"This smells so good. But, I don't want to be rude or anything . . ."

"But?"

"Well, there's something that looks a little like a sea monster in here."

"That would be the squid."

"It would."

"Probably."

"Oh."

"Push it aside if you're too timid and cowardly to try something new."

I gave her a look. I hadn't gotten used to her not being able to read a look like that. "Listen here," I said in my best John Wayne imitation. "Ain't a beast on land or sea that I couldn't wrassle and win. Don't you worry about me, li'l lady. I ain't a-scared."

I huffed, fanning my open mouth.

"A little too hot for you, Duke? Give me your glass."

She reached out her hand and I gave her my glass. She poured in iced tea and stopped exactly one inch from the top. She held it out. I drank half the glass in two gulps.

"I have a question. How do you know when to stop pouring?"

"I can tell by the weight when it's almost full."

Amazing.

We talked about the book, which we both thought was pretty good. As much as I liked reading it to her, talking about it was even better. That was the best part.

We talked for a while more. For some reason, I felt comfortable talking with her. There weren't many adults I felt too much at ease with, none, that I could have named. But there was something about her, the way she talked to me totally straight, not like she was talking to some kid. She wanted to know what I thought. There was just something totally real about her.

It was still kind of strange for me to look at her and know that she couldn't see me. At first I felt like it was unfair, and I tried to not look at her so much, but then I kind of got used to it and looked at her more. I noticed that she had very straight teeth. Her left ear was pierced seven times and had seven different-sized hoops in it. And she had really interesting eyes.

I guess the eyes were what held me. They were bright green and very clear. They moved the way people with vision moved their eyes. They didn't sort of move around unfocused, like I would have expected. It was still kind of hard for me to believe that her eyes couldn't see.

When the kitchen clock tolled eight o'clock, she said she had some things to take care of, that we should call it a night. We went into the living room and I put on my coat.

She had a wallet in her hand.

"I'm going to pay you on Fridays, if that's okay."

"Oh. Sure. Whatever." I had almost forgotten about getting paid.

She opened her wallet and took out money. She handed it to me. The twenties were folded lengthwise, the tens were folded in thirds, the fives were folded in half the short way, and the ones had the corners folded over. "That's seventy-two. Is that all right?"

"It's great. It's too much, though. I can't take it."

"Please. It's what we agreed to. I'm so happy this is working out."

"Me, too."

We made arrangements to meet on Monday. I would have been willing to meet over the weekend, but I figured after the fight with Mom, I should stick around and make sure everything was smoothed out.

I got home feeling stuffed and happy. I put on the TV, not sure what movie I felt like watching. A commercial came on that showed a little boy playing with a bunch of golden retriever puppies, rolling around on a lawn covered with autumn leaves. His sweater-clad father put his arm around the sweater-clad mom; they exchanged a tender look and then gazed happily at junior and the pups. The voice-over asked: "And what will happen if you can't be there?" It ended on a fade to black, with the kid's laughter and the puppies' yelping on the sound track. The screen flashed the 1-800 number and the name of an insurance company.

I got all misty. The very next commercial was for baby

wipes, and it just showed a mother bathing and singing to her little baby. I got an ache in my chest and a real lump in my throat.

I flipped around the channels and struck gold with *The Third Man*. The perfect end for a great day. I waited for the commercial and went into the kitchen for a drink. I got a Dr Pepper and was heading back to Welles when I saw that Mom had left me a note on the kitchen table. She usually left a note if she planned on being out really late or maybe spending time with Hal.

I checked the note to see if I should wait up for her. I put the soda down.

It would have been a long wait.

blur

The note was written on a small, narrow piece of paper that had a brown arc left by the bottom of the coffee cup she used to hold it down.

K—

You're very stubborn and you sometimes really get me angry. You're a smart kid, smarter than me in some ways. But there are a few things that I know more about than you do. You don't know everything. And I still am the adult and you're the kid. And it's the grownups who call the shots. Remember that.

Went on a little trip with Hal. We'll be gone a little longer than usual. I left money you-know-where.

And the ATM card is in the usual place, if you really, really need it. (But don't go crazy with it. Trust me. I'll check!)

I'll call from there. And I'll let you know how great it is. And you'll see how wrong you are.

Do your homework, don't leave the house in just that old sweatshirt— wear your coat. Don't do anything stupid.

See ya. Love,
M.

I should have known she'd do it. She didn't say it in so many words, but she was obvious and she was predictable.

She went to California.

If it had just been the usual weekend trip, she would have said where she was going. But that part, "I'll let you know how great it is," was a pretty clear tip-off. This scheme of a restaurant in L.A. was on her mind and she and Hal wouldn't give it up until they looked into it.

I put the note up on the refrigerator, under a magnet of the poster for the movie *Freaks*. I stood by the counter and looked at the table. The only sounds were the refrigerator humming and the TV in the other room.

"I have your essays." Mr. Brody began to pass them out, facedown. "You outdid yourselves. Overall, I'd say these were actually painful to read. We might be able to sell these to the government for some kind of weapon. But it might be considered too cruel and unusual a punishment to inflict on our enemies."

"Mr. Brody, 'cruel and unusual' is from the Constitution. I think you mean using the papers would violate the Geneva Convention's Rules of Warfare," I said.

"Actually, they would violate any sense of decency, and many laws of God and Man. How's that?"

"So you're saying they weren't too good."

"Ah. See that? You're pretty smart after all," Brody said. "Just out of curiosity, how many of you really read the book? The truth, please."

About half the kids raised their hands. I wasn't one of them.

"Very impressive. I'm so proud of you guys." He shook his head. Nobody seemed too moved either way. He handed back my essay. There was no grade. At the top, he had written "See me." He walked around handing back the rest of the essays. I tuned out when he went over it. He called on me to explain Appearance v. Reality in *Of Mice and Men*. I shrugged and said I didn't know. He gave me a look and endured a nonsense answer from one of the girls before he answered it himself.

I tried to get past him after class, but he grabbed the back of my shirt collar and pulled me back into the room.

"Hey! I don't know if you can do that," I said. "I think I could sue you."

"Go ahead. I'll see you in court. What's going on with you?"

"What do you mean?"

"Why are you pretending that you didn't read the book?"

I shrugged.

"You think I'm an idiot?" he asked.

"No. Not at all."

"Out of curiosity, how much time did you spend writing this?"

"I'm not sure. I didn't keep track."

"Five hours? Five minutes?"

"Somewhere in between."

"If I guessed you spent less than fifteen minutes, would I be far off?"

"Not too."

"That's what I thought. It's really pretty good for a rush job. It barely makes sense, but I could see what you were getting at. The thing is, Kirk, if this is what you can do without even trying, I think you could do phenomenal work if you'd put even a little bit of effort into it."

I looked at him. He looked directly at me. I looked away.

"You have a really interesting mind, Kirk. But you keep hiding it. I can't see what's really going on in your head. I'd like to work with it, to help you, but I can't do squat if you won't talk to me. Think about it."

I nodded. "Thanks. I will." I couldn't remember the last time a teacher had spoken to me like he or she cared at all.

After school, when we got to Glenn's house, he opened the refrigerator. "So, Saint Kirk. Maybe today's the day for you to break your vow off substances?" He held out a beer for me. I looked at it. "You're sure wound up tight enough. Maybe a beer'll do the trick. Or a doobie."

I took a breath. Glenn drank and he smoked pot with Donna. I had no problem with them doing it. I just never did it myself. It wasn't that I had any kind of moral objection to it. It didn't bother me one bit. It's just that in all the years I had watched Mom drink, I never saw it do her any good. It really didn't seem to make her any happier. And I guess I knew that she was hooked. I didn't want that for me.

So I declined the beer and pot. Glenn shrugged and handed me a Pepsi. That was one of the things that I really liked about him: he never pressured me to do stuff like drink or smoke. Live and let live was his thing, and I never appreciated it more than at that moment.

Glenn was working on some slow, bluesy stuff. It was this totally relaxing type of sound. I guess it would sound crazy to say that Glenn was trying to inspire me to write, but the music he was making basically got me completely into my head. And of course that got me thinking about Mom. I got out my notebook and it all came quickly.

It's hard to conceive
How you would leave.
A new leaf to be turned
Should leave me spurned,
But guess again . . .
I'm not so spurnable, burnable, it's
Discernable to me
That the son also rises
To the occasion

Don't try to kid the kid, kid
Keep your persuasion
You have it wrong, you don't understand
Who has the lower, who has the upper hand

"Got a new one?" Glenn asked.

"Working on it," I said. I read it over and I realized that I wasn't sure I wanted to say all that. It wasn't what I thought I believed. But then, why did I write it like that? Where did it come from?

The door upstairs opened and closed. Donna called down the stairs, "You guys working? I brought company."

"Who?" Glenn called up.

"Lauren's here with me."

"Come on down."

I looked up as they came down, Donna first. The person behind her was Parole Girl.

"You know Kirk, right?"

"Yeah, we're in English together. Hi."

"Hi," I said. I was kind of confused. I didn't know that Glenn or Donna knew Parole Girl. "So how do you know each other?" I asked.

"Me and Lauren? We've been like best friends since like—what?—fifth grade?"

"Fourth, I think," Parole Girl said.

"Opener," Donna said. Glenn held the guitar pick between his teeth while he took a bottle opener off the chain he wore that went from his belt loop to his back pocket. He tossed it to Donna, but Parole Girl reached in front of her and snatched it out of the air. Pretty slick. If I tried doing that, I'd miss and get an opener in my teeth. She opened her beer and Donna's beer.

They slouched down in the vinyl chairs.

"What are you working on?" Parole Girl asked.

"Just this twelve-bar blues deal," Glenn said.

"Glenn does the music, Kirk writes the lyrics," Donna said.

"Cool," Parole Girl said. "Let's hear something."

"I'm working this one out. I don't wanna stop right now," Glenn said.

"Well, then let me read something," Parole Girl said. She was looking at me.

"I don't have anything. Glenn has all of it," I said. I didn't much feel like being mocked or whatever she would do when she read my stuff. It was fine that Glenn and Donna liked it, but I knew that it would seem like total nonsense to anyone else.

"Lemme see that, what's in your hand," she said.

"Oh, this is something else," I said.

"Just stop being a baby and let me see it," she said. She got up, came over, and held out her hand.

She stood in front of me when she read it. She squinted and pursed her lips. One hand went up and moved the hair out of her eyes.

"Wow," she said. "You're kind of a poet."

"It's not poetry."

"What is it then?"

"It's just . . . stuff. It's really nothing."

She shrugged. "I think it's good." She dropped the notebook back on my lap.

"So you're not gonna play for us?" Donna asked Glenn.

"I'm workin' on this. It's not a good time now."

"Fine. We're gonna go up and watch TV," Donna said.

"Have fun," Glenn said.

As they went up the stairs, Parole Girl said something to Donna, something I didn't hear. "I *told* you," Donna said back.

Glenn went back to playing chords, and writing down what he had just worked out.

"She's kinda cute, huh?" Glenn said.

"Who, Parole Girl?"

"What?"

It had slipped out. "Lauren?"

"No, what did you just call her?" He looked at me, a big smile on his face.

"Nothing. I said Lauren."

"No, you didn't. You said something else. 'Parole Girl'? What does *that* mean?"

"Nothing. It's stupid. It's just a name I made up for her."

"'Parole Girl'?" Glenn laughed. "Classic. I love it. Lauren!" he bellowed toward the stairs.

"*No!*" I said. "Don't do it!"

"It's too good!" he said. "Donna, Lauren! You gotta hear this!"

"What?" Donna called down.

"I'm serious. Don't," I said.

"What's the matter? It's funny."

"No. She might not think it's funny. She might be insulted. Don't do it."

Glenn looked at me.

"Don't," I said.

"What?" Donna called. "We're watching something."

"Nothing," Glenn called up. He looked at me. "You're something, boy. Anyways, you didn't answer my question. You think she's cute?"

"What are you, my mother? Why don't you worry about your guitar and leave my social life to me. I do fine on my own," I said.

He looked at me and started laughing. I had to look down so he wouldn't see me laugh, too. Then something occurred to me. "Oh, no. What time is it?"

"I dunno, like six?"

"Shit. I totally forgot. I gotta go."

I was glad to get to Callie's house. I had been looking forward to the warmth and good cooking smells all day. She was barefoot and in a light purple short-sleeved shirt. She kept the place very warm. I noticed that all of her clothes were kind of neutral colors: beige, light blue, pale yellow. Pastels, I guess they're called. Using my brilliant powers of deduction, I figured out that her clothes wouldn't clash. You wouldn't need to see them to get them to look right. It was pretty funny that this blind woman could get her clothes to match better than I could.

"If you don't mind, before we get started, there's something else I could use your help with."

"Sure. What can I do?"

"We need to go through my mail. It's over there on the table. We're going to make three groups. One is keeper, one is accountant, one is junk. Read it off to me and I'll tell you where it goes."

I found a big pile of mail on the desk and started reading off to her. It was a pretty big assortment: phone bill (accountant), supermarket mailers (keeper), letter from Patty Farkus (keeper), coupons from Sterling Optical (junk), electric bill (accountant), bank statement (accountant), Victoria's Secret catalog (keeper)(!), offer for trial subscription to *Sports Illustrated* (junk), Kmart coupons (junk), dated reply form from a CD club (keeper). There was some more stuff, most of it total garbage. She said her accountant was coming in the morning and he would deal with the bills. She might ask me to read some of the keepers to her another time. I tried not to dwell on the Victoria's Secret catalog, but it got me wondering a little bit about why she was interested in it. Someone would have to describe the pictures to her. I wondered who that would be, and was she wearing that stuff for herself, or for someone else.

Somehow, I couldn't quite imagine her in that kind of stuff. She seemed kind of a basic person. It's not that she was prudish or uptight or anything like that, but she just didn't seem really sexy in that obvious kind of way. But what did I know about any of that? To tell the truth, I wasn't exactly the world's most experienced lover.

We read *Catch-22* for two hours and talked about it for a while.

"The characters are really pretty goofy, but it's so good," I said.

"I don't usually like stuff that's so broad, you know?

It's very far removed from reality, but somehow it works," Callie said.

Far removed from reality. Tell me about it. I kept realizing at different times in the day that it was so weird how I was going about life like nothing had changed, like everything was normal, when in reality, Mom up and left me and was chasing her ridiculous idea about moving us to California. "The situation is insane and it applies to all of us. It's an absurd world." I couldn't have said whether I was talking about the book or about life.

"And on that note . . ." Callie said.

She had made chicken paprika, which she said was a Hungarian chicken stew. It was a deep color, sort of a reddish-orange, a little spicy, and all-around really good. I was starting to understand that her dishes were always some kind of stew or soup, which I guess was easier for her to cook than individual kinds of things.

"Just out of curiosity, did you feed Janet when she read to you?"

"Nope."

"How come?"

"Janet was mostly all business. She came to read and that was basically it. Don't get me wrong. She read well, and that really was what I hired her for, but she wasn't much of a socializer. And she had a family to go home to."

"Right. I hear the baby is cute. I haven't seen it."

"Me either," Callie said. I looked at her. She smiled in my direction. "So what about *your* family?"

"Well, it's just me and my mom."

"Dad?"

"Took off when I was a babe. He took one look at me and ran for the hills."

"Stop."

"Hey, you haven't seen me."

"I don't expect to anytime soon. I have a feeling you're very handsome."

"Don't rely on your feelings too much, then."

"They haven't failed me yet. So your father left. Are you mad about that?"

"Mad? No. I mean, it's all I've ever known. It's just part of my life. There's really nothing to be mad about. It's the way it is."

"So it's just you and your mom."

"Two of a kind."

"You're close?"

"Sure. We kind of have to be. Being just us alone, we need to rely on each other."

"Sticking together through thick and thin, and all that."

"Pretty much."

"That's nice. Did you want some more to eat?"

"No, I'm stuffed, thanks."

"I hope she won't be mad at me for ruining your appetite."

"I wouldn't worry about it. What about your family?"

"Just me, myself, and I."

"Really?"

"Well, my parents died a while back. I have a sister in Chicago, but we don't speak too much. Holidays, a few times a year, that's it. I'm pretty much on my own."

We sat in silence for a while. I tried to think of something to say but couldn't come up with anything. She wore a thin silver ring with a dark stone, and she was turning it around and around on her finger. Her hands were small, but she had long, thin fingers. They looked like they should be playing beautiful songs or classical music on the violin or the piano.

"Do you play any kind of musical instrument?" I asked.

"No. I have the worst sense of rhythm. Why?"

"Just asking."

"Anyway, I don't want to keep you too late. Your mom is probably wondering where you are."

"Oh, I doubt it. She knows I'm close to home."

It was dark when I got home, and there was a sparkle of frost on our car, which Mom left parked in front of the house. A lot of kids would have been tempted to get the spare key that was kept in the kitchen drawer and go driving, but not me. I didn't want to take the chance of getting caught and losing my learner's permit and having to wait even longer to get my license. I would only drive if I really had to.

It was dark in the house. I had left the light on in the living room all night and I left it on when I left in the morning, but it burned out. Suddenly, I got this totally creepy feeling, like my heart started pounding and I felt that electric feeling in my body.

I rushed toward the kitchen and banged my knee on the coffee table. I cursed and hobbled into the kitchen and hit the lights. I let out a long breath and started laughing. I didn't know what I was laughing about, maybe about being such a dope.

"There we have it, folks. The kid has flipped out," I announced in a game show host's voice. I opened the broom closet to get a bulb for the living room. On the counter next to the closet was the place where Mom kept her bottles. I picked up a bottle of Johnny Walker Red.

When I was a little kid, I used to look at the empty bottles she'd leave on the coffee table. I used to look at the picture of Johnny Walker on the label, this dandy with his monocle marching off somewhere, grinning. I liked him. I wondered why he was so happy. The look on his face made me imagine that he knew some funny secret, some inside joke. Looking at the same picture years later, I understood what he thought was so funny. I got the joke, but it wasn't too funny to me.

There were a couple of inches of scotch left. I tilted it. I took it to the back door, off the kitchen. We have a small bit of woods between us and the house behind. I stood in the doorway, my silhouette framed by a rectangle of light on the frosted grass. I held the bottle by the neck and raised it. "Here's to you and Hal, Mom," I said. I picked a big tree and aimed. I threw the bottle as hard as I could, right at the tree. I missed. Instead of the dramatic shatter I was looking for, I got a dull thud in the dark.

I looked into Mom's room when I got upstairs. She almost never was in her room when I went to bed. She might have been downstairs, or she might have been out.

I went into my room and got into bed.

I couldn't figure out why I had thrown the bottle, why

I wanted it to shatter. But it didn't break, and it would just sit there. If I didn't remember to go get it, when Mom got back, she might see it from the kitchen window and ask me how that bottle got out there in the woods.

I wouldn't have an answer.

The house was totally silent in the morning. It was usually pretty silent, since I was always the first one up. Still, this was a different kind of silence. It was the silence of absence. Yes, she had gone away before, but she never went as far away as California, and she'd never gone with any kind of plan or idea. So even though she had always come back after a few days, this time I really didn't know how long she was going to be away.

I had left her bedroom door open, and I made an effort not to look in when I passed to go to the bathroom. I actually turned my head and looked the other way. I felt like a little kid turning away from a scary picture in a book, trying to quickly turn the page and move on.

Hard as it was to believe, that morning I was eager to get to school. I just wanted out of the house.

I didn't bother to pay attention in most of my classes. My notes looked like EKG readouts. Sorry, Doc, but we're losing this patient.

"What do I have in common with a surgeon who has shaky hands?" Mr. Brody asked.

Several heads lifted up. There was interest in anything that was going to break the monotony for the numskulls in the class.

"We're both losing our patience," he said. Like a good comic, he didn't wait for a response, probably because he knew most of them wouldn't get the pun. "You guys need to read the book. I'm pretty sure that if you'd give it a chance, you'd like it."

"I thought the part where they shoot Candy's dog was kind of powerful." It was Lauren speaking. I looked over. I couldn't remember ever hearing her speak in class. I had been thinking a little about her since we met in Glenn's basement. I watched her.

"In what way?" Brody asked.

"Well, not in the way that you'd think," she said. "It's not just 'aw, gee, it's so sad that this old guy gets convinced to let the other ranch workers kill his old worn-out dog.' Nobody could find a reason for his existence anymore. You could say that all the other characters felt a little like the dog. They were pretty much useless. The bloodthirsty guy said something like, the dog's no use to himself, but that wasn't the point. They wouldn't admit it, but the world kind of treated these *people* as useless trash. Nobody gave a fuck about them."

Well, that got the attention of a bunch of the kids who loved it when someone would curse in class. It wasn't the cursing that got me. It was the angry look on her face. You'd think she was talking about people she knew personally.

"Let's try to keep this at a PG-13 level, okay?"

"Fine. Nobody gave a shit about them, and it was just a matter of luck that nobody bothered to take them out and shoot them, too."

"Okay," Mr. Brody said. "Hold that thought for the end of the book. Since nobody read, again, take out your books, read up to page ninety-six and write an outline, so I know you're really reading."

I watched Lauren take out her book and pen. I had my head lowered, making sure that it looked like I was reading. But I had my eye on her.

We were in the parking lot, walking to Glenn's car.

"That was pretty good, what Lauren said in class, huh?" I said.

"I dunno. I wasn't listening."

"Really? She had this really interesting idea."

"You have to know that I'm not listening to you."

"She's pretty smart, huh?"

"Who, Parole Girl?"

"All right. God. Forget I said that. Lauren. She's pretty smart."

"I guess."

"I think she might be. She got something that nobody else in the class got. Not that that's such a huge accomplishment in that group, but still. She seems different, don't you think?"

"She's pretty different, yeah."

I looked up at him. He pulled his black wool cap lower on his head. He was looking at the pavement in front of him as he walked.

"Hm," I said, not really knowing how to bring it up. We got to Glenn's car and he started to get his keys. "What do you think, you think there's any chance that she—"

"Why don't you ask her. She's right over there."

"What?" I looked over and saw her walking with some girls I didn't know.

"Just ask her out."

"No, that's not what I was going to say."

"Hey, Lauren! Come here."

"Shut up!" I said. "What are you doing?"

"Live dangerously, Slick."

I grabbed the door handle to escape, but Glenn hadn't unlocked my side yet.

"What's up?" Lauren asked.

"He was just talking about you," Glenn said. I looked at him. He smiled. Jeez. I turned to her.

"I liked what you said in class. About the dog."

"I think we're the only ones who even read the damned thing."

"Yeah. So it would seem." Oh my God. Who was I trying to be, British Royalty? *So it would seem?* "Well, I thought your comment was good. You're a George in a class full of Lennies."

"Ha."

"Well, anyway, see ya later." I tried to force a smile, which I just knew was coming off crooked and made me feel like a maniac. I started yanking at the door handle, but it wouldn't open. I looked at Glenn over the roof of the car. He smiled at me and slowly shook his head.

I gave him a look. He shook his head again, gave a little nod toward Lauren. I looked at him again. He shrugged and raised his eyebrows.

Later, I'd dump a bucket of water over him and his damned guitar, electrocute the guy. I took a breath and turned to Lauren.

"So, the thing of it is, I was wondering if, maybe." My voice did this kind of gulping thing and it was kind of hard to get the words out. It must have seemed like I was having some kind of seizure or something. "I thought it might be a good idea, pretty, you know, cool, if maybe, we could go out sometime. Together. Maybe."

"Sure."

"What?"

"Sounds good. Lemme know. I gotta run."

She smiled, which I hadn't seen her do too much before. It really changed her whole look. Not to say that her other look was so bad. She went back to her girlfriends. I heard the click of the door locks.

"You're dead," I said when I got in the car. Glenn grinned at me.

"What?" I asked.

"I'm proud of you, son. You got yourself a little girl-friend."

"She definitely seems to like me, right?"

"Who wouldn't? You're so smooth."

"Me?"

"I thought you were going to faint." He cornered the turn hard enough to throw me against the door. My luck, I'd fall out and get run over by a truck before my date.

"Listen. I'll tell you the truth," I confided. "I haven't really had a lot of girlfriends before."

"Really? You're kidding."

I finished reading a chapter of *Catch-22* and looked up. I would have sworn Callie was looking right into my eyes.

"What's the matter?" she asked.

"Huh? Nothing, I just . . . Nothing."

"You stopped reading." The light hit her eyes, made them look electric green. They looked totally focused.

"Sorry. I just looked up for a second," I said.

"More like a minute."

"Oh. Well. I'll tell you the truth. The way you're . . . the way you look? I don't know how to say this, but, I mean, it's just hard to believe that you can't see anything."

"Who said I can't see *any*thing?"

"Well, wait. You told me you're blind."

"Functionally, I am. But I can see light and dark. Hints of big shapes."

"Really?"

"For all the good it does me. I can't read. I can't identify people by the way they look. I can't see whether someone is smiling or sneering. I can't see the fingers on my own hand. It's still called blind."

"I had no idea. So you can see me. When you're looking at me, you actually see me."

"Not really. I don't know what you look like."

"Well, what do I look like to you?"

"Honestly? You look like a smudge. You look like a blur."

I put on the TV and spent an hour working on a script for a phone call to Lauren.

ME: Hi, Lauren. It's Kirk Tobak.
HER: Who?
or
ME: Hey, Lauren. It's Kirk. Tobak.
HER: Hi.
ME: Remember we talked about going out?
HER: Oh, sure. That was pretty funny, right? I just said that to get Glenn jealous.
ME: You what?
HER: Well, I have this wicked crush on Glenn, even though he's with my friend, I still think about being with him. He's so great, and good-looking, and cool. So I thought maybe the way to get him would be to say that I would go out with the guy who's most opposite to him and that, of course, is *you*!

After a while, I realized I needed a better screenwriter for my life than myself, and decided to give it a rest.

But I was making myself nuts, buzzing with energy. I couldn't sit, but I wasn't ready to call her. I found an old B-movie about an invasion from outer space. For the life of me, I couldn't remember the name, but the dialogue was so bad and so predictable that I turned down the volume and had a pretty good time supplying the words myself.

"'But Chet, whatever do they want from us?' 'Why, they want our minds, Nancy. They want our minds and our very souls! Don't they, Professor?' 'I'm afraid Chet's right, Nancy. It is pointless to resist. They're a much more sophisticated species than we are. I almost . . . admire them.'"

I could have stayed up all night doing that. But I was interrupted when the phone rang. Probably Glenn. But what if it was her? What if Lauren decided not to wait, to call me before I chickened out? I didn't have my script done. I hadn't even gotten to a decent first draft.

Just be cool, I thought. Go easy. Think Clark Gable, think Errol Flynn, think Cary Grant. Charisma, baby. You can talk to this girl.

I let out a breath and picked up the phone.

"Alien Headquarters," I said. "Your home planet is our home planet. Skirk speaking, may I help you?"

"That's a pretty strange way to answer the phone."

I was wrong. It wasn't Lauren. And it wasn't Glenn.

It was Mom.

"Where are you?" I asked.

"Well, I'm at a motel outside of L.A."

"No kidding. A motel. Sounds really classy."

"How are you doing?" Chet, Nancy, and the Professor hid in a doorway as the invading force moved past them. The Professor's nice white lab jacket had gotten dirty.

"Fine. Totally fine. So, how are things out in La-La Land?"

"Pretty good. I have lots of good news."

"Really."

"We saw the restaurant. It's going to be fantastic. I didn't realize it, but it's in this area that's suddenly becoming very trendy."

The aliens saw the heroes and started chasing them. The professor stumbled.

"Trends end, you know," I said.

"I'm not worried about it. Hal is pretty sharp about this kind of stuff."

Yeah, Hal is sharp. Sharp as a gumdrop.

"And the other good thing is we think we found a place."

The Professor couldn't walk anymore. Chet wouldn't leave him behind. He swung the Professor's arm over his shoulder and dragged him along. The Professor wanted to believe he'd be okay. Chet would humor him.

"No kidding. What kind of a place?" I asked.

"It's not huge, I guess a lot smaller than the house. It's a little apartment and it doesn't really have views or much furniture. But it's clean. It's conveniently located."

"Sounds spectacular."

"It's a start. I think this'll work out fine."

"No kidding."

"No kidding. What's the tone for?"

"You want to know?"

"Yes, I want to know."

"Fine. I'll tell you. I think this is the stupidest idea I've ever heard. You don't uproot your whole life and your kid's life and everything just to follow some guy across the country to be a waitress in some crappy restaurant."

"Hostess."

"Whatever. Big difference."

There was a silence, a three-thousand mile silence. Chet had gotten hold of a machine gun, and he was silently blasting the aliens to bits. They had Nancy hostage, but Chet was a good shot. He was a marksman.

"So that's what you think."

"That's what I think."

"Well, I'm sorry to hear that. I'm sorry to hear that you have no confidence in me and that you don't believe in trying to make good things happen."

"I'm trying to be realistic. Come on. Be responsible."

"You're telling me how to be responsible?"

"Someone has to."

There was a silence on the phone line. I wondered if there was any chance she could hear my heart beating. It sure was beating hard enough. I took a long breath, hoping it would calm me down. I summoned the most reasonable tone of voice I could. "You need to come home."

"You need to come here."

"This is where we live."

"Not anymore. I'm not coming back."

"Well, I'm not going out there."

There was a long silence.

"I don't know what to say," she said.

"Me either."

"This isn't how I wanted this to go."

"Me either."

"You're very stubborn."

"I wonder where I get it from."

I realized I was breathing pretty heavily, deep in the chest. My heart thundered.

"This is what they call a deadlock," I said.

"Looks like it. You're not going to change your mind?"

"No."

"Me either."

Another long silence. The phone felt slippery in my hand. The tighter I gripped it, the harder it was to hold.

"I have to go," she said. "I'll call."

"See ya."

I listened for a moment. We waited each other out to see who would hang up first. It was almost funny. Except it really wasn't.

I heard a click.

I held the receiver in my hand for a moment, then slammed it down, harder than I wanted to. The crack echoed through the house.

Chet had saved everybody. But that was the movie.

The movie was over.

Fade to black.

hooked up

When I was about nine, Mom got it into her head that we could use a weekend getaway. She rented us a house down on the Jersey shore for a long weekend. The only problem, as I saw it, was that the beach wasn't the perfect place to go in late October. Still, it was away, was her point. It would be nice. We could make a fire in the fireplace, spend some time away from our place. It was a getaway.

I was pretty doubtful, but I went along for the ride, as they say. It turned out that I was right. The house was drafty and cold. The carpets smelled of mildew. The whole place was damp. I didn't exactly help her feel better about her plan. She kept trying to be cheery and make it seem like we were having fun, and I just looked at her and shrugged. I knew at the time that I was being a pain, but I was hoping, at best, that she'd realize this was a rotten idea and we'd go home, or at least, that I would make her feel rotten for having a rotten idea and sticking to it. Looking back, I must have been a pretty obnoxious little kid.

Late in the afternoon of the first day, I was going out of my mind from playing Monopoly and Rummy-Q with her. I said I was going to take a walk on the beach. She said she'd come along.

"I'd rather have some private time," I said. It was a trump card. Whenever I said that, she somehow felt it was something almost sacred, that a kid would want some private time. She felt she should respect it.

So I went for a walk on the beach. There were two boys near the surf. They were twins, almost identical, and probably a year younger than me, though they were much taller. They were looking out at a small wooden boat that had capsized and was bobbing in the water just past the breakers. They looked at me, then back at the boat.

"How'd it get out there?" I asked.

"We got it out, but the string broke," one of the twins said. "It isn't coming back."

"That's too bad."

"We could get it. I could run out."

"The water's gotta be cold," I pointed out.

They looked miserable. "We gotta get it back, though," Twin B said.

We watched the hull of the boat bob up and down for a while. Twin A kicked off his sneakers, rolled up his pants legs and started to step out into the water. A wave hit him and knocked him over. He got up laughing. "It's cold!" he shrieked. It looked like too much fun to pass up. A couple of minutes later, all of us were sitting in the sand, letting the freezing water splash up against our chests. After a while, I noticed that it was starting to get dark, and I decided I'd better get back.

My jeans were stiff with the cold seawater and they made a shuff-shuff-shuff sound, the legs rubbing against each other as I stiff-walked across the sand back to the house.

When I pulled the door closed, I heard her call out from the small bedroom, "Is that you?" and she came out quickly. "What happened to you?"

"I was in the ocean."

"What? Why?"

"Just playing," I said.

"What?" She looked at me and she started shaking. She grabbed my shoulders and shook me. "Playing? In the ocean in October? Are you out of your mind? Do you know what could have happened?" Her head started to shake and her lips turned in. She slapped me, pretty hard, across the cheek.

"You could have drowned!" she said, her voice loud, but wavering.

I cupped my hand under my chin and spit into my palm. In the middle of the spit was a swirl of blood and a tooth.

"Well I didn't," I said. I dropped the tooth on the floor, wiped my hand on my jeans, and went into the bathroom and shut the door.

Time to set the record straight. She had never hit me before, and this wasn't exactly the knockout blow it might have seemed. The tooth had been loose; I had actually been twisting it in the afternoon to work it even looser. But I knew enough at that point to know that I could get some undeserved mileage out of letting her think she had knocked the tooth out. I sat in the tub, trying to pump up my outrage at her hitting me, and to push back the guilt at having worried her and the stupidity of what I had done. I knew I was wrong, really, but I was going to let her take the final rap for the whole thing. I could have told her about the tooth being loose, but if she felt bad enough about hitting me, then I might be able to miss out on a lecture or punishment, or her anger.

I went straight from the bathroom into my little bedroom. The sheets were gritty with sand. After a while, there was a soft knock on the door.

"Yeah," I grumbled.

The door opened and she stood there. She had a hard time meeting my eyes. This weekend had been her great idea, I had been against it, and for whatever reason, it had been a disaster. On top of it she had hit me, hurt me.

I thought about that time after I hung up with Mom. I knew how to play her. I could have made her feel guilty about leaving like that. But I didn't need to do it. I knew that the whole thing was going to backfire on her. Something was going to happen. It might be that the restaurant wouldn't work out, or it would turn out to suck. Or Hal would start messing with some girl. My bet was that he wouldn't get through the weekend without trying to make it with some young, blond California girl. Mom would see what a disastrous idea it was and she'd come home. Maybe she wouldn't be happy about it at first, but she would have gotten this whole thing out of her system, and she'd come back home.

This would be no problem at all. It would just be like she had taken another little vacation. Nothing to worry about for me. I would be on vacation, too.

Before first period, I passed Glenn and Donna in the hall. She had her back against a locker. He was leaning toward her, his hands on the locker. She had her hands deep in the back pockets of his jeans. He was talking to her, his mouth close to her ear. She was nodding and smiling. I never saw them into heavy making out at the lockers in school, like a lot of the other kids, the jocks and cheerleaders, for example. Glenn and Donna had too much class for that. I watched him talking to her, the way she comfortably held onto him, so relaxed. The word I came up with was intimate. That was it, comfortably intimate.

I wanted that with a girl. I wanted to have a girlfriend that I could talk to and hang around with. A girlfriend who I could be comfortably intimate with, that was what I really wanted. To be totally honest, I really spent a lot of time wishing for that. It seemed like just about the best thing to have, a girlfriend who you felt that way about. Maybe it would finally happen for me.

Glenn had to go to a guitar shop that was about six towns over, like twenty-five minutes away, and he dragged me along.

"Look at that Strat, man. Is that cool, or what?" he said.

"It's so cool, I feel like I'm having a religious experience," I said.

"I'm starting to regret bringing you," Glenn said.

"Oh, no. Really? I was hoping we'd come here every day after school."

"What do *you* know? Look at all these beautiful guitars. That one. That is one wicked cool ax. Can't afford that one, either."

"What are we doing here?" I asked him.

"I need a new pickup. Where's the guy, anyways? Excuse me, could you give me a hand?"

A skinny guy with an impossibly long and stringy goatee came over. Glenn asked to see the guitar he liked so much, and then explained what kind of pickup he wanted. The guy said he had them in the back and disappeared.

Glenn noodled around with the guitar. It sounded tinny not plugged in. Still, Glenn made it sound pretty good.

"Hey," I said. "Speaking of pickups. Since you're Mister Romance, maybe you could give me some advice."

"Yeah, sure, I'm Mister Romance. What?"

"So I was going to ask Lauren out, but to tell you the truth, I don't really know what to do with her."

"You kidding? Take her to a movie. That's the obvious first date choice, right?"

"Well, sure. But is that too much for a first date?"

"What? What are you talking about? You're sitting in a dark theater."

Two younger kids, burnouts-in-training, who were playing with an amp nearby stopped to watch Glenn play little solo stuff up and down the guitar.

"Well, that's what I mean. I'm just saying, is it going to seem like, 'Whoa, this guy is trying to get me to a dark theater and he's going to try to put the moves on me or something?' Is it going to seem that way?"

Glenn stopped playing and looked at me. "Are you for real? What planet are you from?"

"I don't know. I just don't want it to seem like I'm trying to, you know . . ."

"Ya know, I think there's really something wrong with you. Why do you always act like such a weirdo?"

"Who's acting?"

"She likes you. She's wants to go out with you. She's cool. Why do you have to, like, second-guess everything?"

"I don't know." I ran my fingers through a bin of slippery plastic guitar picks. It should have been embarrassing to admit it, since most guys my age had had girlfriends before. But I felt it would be okay to tell Glenn. "I'm not really experienced. Ya know?"

He nodded. "That's okay. Just be cool and give yourself a break. Let it happen."

I scooped up a handful of the picks and let them flutter like flower petals back down into the bin. It was good to have a friend like Glenn, a guy I could talk to about girls and things.

The guy came back with the pickups. "You taking the guitar, too?"

"Yeah, I wish," Glenn said. He handed it back like he was handing over his own child.

The parking lot looked like someone was using it for a glass bottle recycling center.

"So let me just ask one more time, and then I'll leave you alone. You think a movie is definitely the way to go? She won't get the wrong idea?"

"Listen, stud. It doesn't even matter where you go. That girl has no chance. She won't be able to control herself when she's around you. She'll totally lose control of herself."

"More likely she'll lose control of her anti-reflux reflex."

"What does that mean?"

"It means I'll probably make her throw up," I said, shards of glass crunching like cereal under my sneakers.

After reading, Callie and I went into the kitchen where she gave me a bowl of pasta fagioli and great bread. "Oh, listen. Could you tell me what mail I have?" Callie asked.

I went to the desk and brought the mail into the kitchen. Like before, she called out "keeper" or "junk" or "accountant" as I read off what she had. It was mostly ads and bills.

"Looks like a card from, hmm, hard to read this. I think it's Tod Barndon?"

"Tod . . . Ted Burnham?"

"Right. That's it. Bad handwriting."

"Junk."

"Really? It looks like a personal thing. A greeting card."

"It's junk. Throw it away. What else?"

"Coupons from Scarlatti's Restaurant. 'The best pizza, pasta, and vino around' it says."

"I don't think so. Junk it."

"I'm not convinced either. Last one: a brochure thingy from B-Gone Pest Control."

"Junk."

"Yeah, they're not too good. My mom hired them. They got rid of our bugs, but they couldn't get rid of me."

"How about that. Did she get her money back?"

"Hmm. Yes she did, but only because she kept bugging them."

"Oh, bad." She tore off a piece of the bread in her hand and threw it with perfect aim at the center of my forehead.

"Hey, fine. More food for me," I said.

"Your mother probably called the pest control people because you were eating her out of house and home. I've never seen anything like it." It took me a little bit by surprise when Callie would say things like that.

"I don't eat like this at home, believe me."

"You're going to put on weight, reading to me." She didn't say anything for a moment. "Tell me, are you heavy?"

I laughed. "Me? Are you kidding?"

"Well, how exactly would I know?"

"That's true. Well, I'm about as big as a fetus."

She laughed. Boy, did Callie have the best laugh. She put her head back, her eyes shined, and the bridge of her nose kind of crinkled. And the sound came from deep in her chest, like from her center, like from her heart. This is what people must really mean by a hearty laugh.

She shook her head and looked at me. I mean, she didn't look at me look at me, but she Callie-looked at me.

"What," I said.

"Nothing. You're fun to be with. You must be very pop-ular in school."

Now it was my turn to laugh.

"What's funny?"

"Well, popular is not exactly how I'd put it. I guess I have a pretty small circle of slightly disturbed and demented friends."

"Do tell."

"Well, there's this guy Glenn and his girlfriend Donna. They're really kind of interesting. Kids like them are sometimes called 'burnouts.' You know what that means?"

"Yes, I know what that means. I'm not a hundred years old."

"That's not what I meant. Anyway, that's pretty much what I thought about them at first. But then I got to know them and they're not at all what I thought they'd be like. They're really good people, good friends."

"How'd you connect with them?"

"Well, Glenn is a really excellent guitar player. And he likes this stuff I write and he wanted to use it for lyrics. We got to be kind of friends."

"Wait a second. What stuff that you write?"

"Oh, it's really nothing. It's just this crazy stuff."

"So when are you going to read some of this to me?"

"What? No, you don't understand. It's just goofy, ram-bling stuff."

"I see. So it's good enough for this guy Glenn, but not for me?"

"No. Yes. You're not . . . I don't know how to put it."

"I'd like to hear your writing."

"It really couldn't be called writing. It's like . . . I don't know. It's like spewings from my weird little mind. Just stupid stuff."

"I'll tell you what," she said. "When you write something you're happy with, you'll read it to me. Fair?"

"Fair enough," I said.

> Fair enough, a fair fare, a fair price to incur.
> My mindless musings are too confusing,
> Immature for a person like her
> And if I read it, I'd have to bet it
> Would expose me as a big poseur.

The next day I paid zero attention to what was going on in school, mainly because I was working out my plans for asking Lauren out. When I got home, I took a shower. It was partly a stall tactic, and partly because somehow I thought that if I felt presentable, I would have the confidence I needed to not make a total ass of myself on the phone.

I spent over an hour pumping myself up to dial her number. This is ridiculous, I tried to tell myself. She wants you, she made that clear. Just do it, pick up that phone and do it.

Her father answered.

"Hello. This is Kirk Tobak. May I please speak to Lauren?"

"Hang on. Lauren!" I heard him yell. I could hear her

ask who is it. "Kurt Somebody," her father said.

"Hello?"

"Hi, Lauren. It's Kirk," I said. No response. "From school?"

"Oh, hi. I thought my stepfather said 'Kurt' and I was trying to think of who I know named Kurt. Hi."

"Hi. So. That was really a pretty boring English class today, huh?"

"Oh, I thought it was okay. I like the book."

"Me, too. Yeah, it was really pretty interesting."

"I thought you said it was boring."

"Well I meant it was so interesting that it went full circle to being boring." At that point, I would have driven a spike through my tongue and shot myself, in that order, if I had had a spike and a gun. "Oh, so, anyway. You know, the reason I'm calling is, that remember when you said maybe we could go out and do something? Remember you said that?" I realized that I sounded like the prosecutor trying to trap a witness in her own words.

"I don't remember that, exactly."

"Well, you did. You said it. You said we might go out or something." Way to go, counselor. Force her into the date. By God, we had a verbal contract!

"Okay. I believe you. I mean, are you asking me out for real?"

"If you want to put it like that, I guess." Damn the torpedoes, son. "I'm asking you out for real."

"Great."

"Great, meaning yes? You mean yes?"

"Uh-huh. I mean yes."

"Okay. Okay. Good. So, I was thinking maybe a movie? Something like that?"

"When?" she asked.

"As soon as . . . whenever it's, you know, convenient. I mean, soon. Let's go, what, Friday, maybe?"

"Okay."

"Friday. Perfect."

At that point I became kind of hyper, listing from memory all the movies playing and telling her a little bit about them, including cast, director, and basic premise. It's a miracle she didn't try to back out of the whole thing.

For some reason, though, she didn't. Hard as it was to believe, this crazy girl actually seemed to want to go out with me.

Lauren smiled at me in English in a way that even I couldn't misinterpret. There was no way I could read anything into it except that she liked me and was still going to go out with me. I stayed pretty quiet all day, trying to keep a low profile.

Rations were pretty low at home, so I needed to go to the market after school. I took the forty dollars Mom left for me. I didn't think it would be enough, so I stopped at the bank and used the debit card Mom had left me. I checked the account and it said $884.93. That seemed like a pretty decent amount. I also had my own account with about half that. I took out another forty bucks and walked to the market.

I leaned on the cart, moving up and down the aisles. I

was hungry, so I might not have been the smartest shopper. I started with three cans of jumbo pitted olives, sandwich pickles, two bags of tortilla chips, baked beans, three bottles of soda, four different kinds of cereal. I put three cans of SpaghettiOs in the cart, and then I decided that it was ridiculous to eat that crap. Why not make spaghetti from scratch? A lot of people did that. I could do it, too. I went down the aisle and picked up a box of spaghetti and a jar of sauce. If they could cook, so could I.

I had a hard time walking home with all of the stuff. One of the plastic bags broke and I had to abandon two bottles of soda. I set them up by the side of the road. Someone could have them.

"I have bad news," I told Callie the next night.

"What's wrong?"

"We're almost at the end of the book."

"Wow. That went fast. We'll have to pick something to start next week."

"Your choice," I said. "Listen, if it's okay, I kind of need to leave a little early tonight."

"Really? Sure. Did you want to try the minestrone I have?"

"I'm gonna take a Pasadena on that this time."

"What? I forgot to listen to the weather. Did hell freeze over? Are you saying no to my food?"

"Well, it's that I have dinner plans. It's a date, really."

"Well, well, well." She sat up and shook out her hand like she burned it. I would swear on my life that she saw me perfectly as she smiled that way. "And what's her name?"

"Lauren."

"Uh-huh. And how long have you been together?"

"It's basically a first date. We're not really together."

"Not yet," she said, smiling.

I felt my ears get hot. A Zen embarrassment riddle: If you blush and nobody can see you, are you blushing?

Once I got home, I took a superlong shower and washed my hair three times. I got dressed on the first try. Not counting the four practice ones, they were just warm-ups to check what matched.

The plan was that Glenn and Donna were going to come with us and we were going to split up and see separate movies. I had said it was okay if we all went to the same movie, but Glenn just clapped me on the shoulder and said it was time for me to leave the nest and fly solo.

So Glenn and Donna picked me up at seven, and on the way to pick up Lauren, Glenn gave me his version of a pep talk.

"She's not shy, but if I were you, I'd still go easy."

"Meaning what?"

"Meaning don't maul her on the first date."

"You think I don't know anything? Okay, don't answer. What should I talk to her about?"

"You never have much of a problem thinking of things to talk about. I wouldn't worry about that. Just be yourself."

"Really? You sure about that?"

"You're right. Better be somebody else."

It occurred to me that Glenn thought he was kidding, but really it was true. My best shot was to not be myself. Being myself hadn't been working so great for me so far. Only problem was, I really didn't know how to be anybody else.

We picked up Lauren and she gave me a big smile when she hopped into the back seat. They all talked about some girl they knew who was rumored to be pregnant. We went to the pizza place next to the multiplex.

Lauren didn't really say much while we ate. I was working hard not to let the cheese pull into long webs between the slice and my mouth. I was totally focused on avoiding any disgusting mishaps and just getting the pizza out of the way as fast as possible. I finished mine as she was starting. Somehow, she didn't look as tough here as she did in school. It must have been my imagination, but it seemed like her expression was a little gentler. Maybe she was more relaxed. Which was pretty funny to me, since I was about as nervous and jittery as I could remember being in a long time.

We talked about movies for a while. I said that I had read a lot about the one I was seeing with Lauren. "I don't know that much about it, except that the script was from this book that got published after the author was tragically killed in a motorcycle accident. I say tragic because he was like twenty-five. Not that all motorcycle deaths aren't tragic, but I guess it's especially tragic when the person is young," I said. Lauren nodded. "You notice how the younger a person is, the more tragic they say it is when they die? Like middle-aged people or old folks don't feel pain, or have regrets, or things they still wanted to do. But I guess it's about unrealized potential or something. I don't know, you know?"

"I know."

We split up after we got our tickets. I caught Glenn's eye. He knew I was a little nervous, and he gave me a thumbs-up.

We were watching the coming attractions and there was a bunch of guys in varsity jackets from another high school sitting up front. They were making loud comments, hooting, and generally acting like jackasses.

Lauren leaned over to me. "Boys who hang and bang, churn and burn, they leave wreckage in their wake. Call the EMT, they are the empty."

My "Howl" riff. I couldn't believe it. "How did you remember that?"

"It stuck with me," she said.

I didn't know what to say.

I looked at her a few times during the movie. Her eyes were turned upward and the light from the screen lit them up, images dancing on her eyes.

When the part came on where the guy is about to get on the motorcycle for the fateful ride, Lauren moved her hand to the armrest. I thought about it, I really debated it, and I just took the chance. I put my hand over hers. She turned her hand over and wrapped her fingers in mine.

We were hooked up.

———

After we dropped Lauren off, Donna turned in the seat to face me.

"So how'd it go?"

"Pretty great."

"Yeah?"

"Yeah."

I leaned back and put my hands behind my head. Glenn looked at me in the rearview mirror.

"Oh, God. Look at him. I can't take it. He's gonna be impossible."

"Hey. I was a natural, babe."

"Jesus. A hobbit stud."

Late that night, Mom called again.

"How are you doing?" she asked.

"I'm doing just fine."

"Are you?"

"Yup. Fine and dandy."

"So are we. You'd love it here. Guess how warm it is here?"

"A thousand degrees."

"It's eighty-two. I'm wearing shorts in December. Hal is sitting across from me in a tank top and a bathing suit."

"Wait, is that image supposed to entice me to come out there?" I wondered if she knew what the word emetic meant.

"I'm saying it's gorgeous. It's fantastic. I want you to come and just see what it's like out here."

"No thanks."

"Just come for a week. During the break."

"I don't think so."

"Well, I'm sending you a plane ticket."

"Don't bother. I'm not using it."

"This is ridiculous."

"I agree. Sending a plane ticket will be a total waste of money, because I am absolutely not coming to California."

"If you're waiting for me to come home—"

"I'm not."

"You don't understand," I heard the sound of ice cubes clinking in a glass, a glass tilted up near the phone. "I know you think I'm doing this on some kind of whim. But you're wrong. I'm trying to do something here. I've wasted my whole damned life in that goddamned town and I'm sick to death of it. I can make this work. I can make it happen. If you think I'm just giving up and coming back, think again."

"Well you know what? I have a life here that's finally decent. I have all good stuff happening. I have friends. A great job. A girlfriend."

"Really?"

"Yes, really." Close, anyway.

"What's her name?"

"It doesn't matter, that's not what we're talking about. I am not coming to California to be a part of a crazy scheme. Forget it. It's totally ridiculous."

"I'm trying to make a decent, interesting life for us out here. For us, for all of us. I want everyone to be happy."

"So do I. Everyone *should* be happy. They just might have to do it in different ways, in different places."

After I hung up with Mom, I slouched into the couch. It was weird to think how it was cold where I was, and dark out already, and at that exact same moment in time, Mom was somewhere where it was warm and sunny.

Then I remembered what Mr. Brody said, sometimes things weren't what they appeared to be. Sure, it might be beautiful and warm and new out there, and it was basically pretty cold and dreary in our rundown dreary house in our rundown dreary town. But Hal was in L.A., and countless other people I didn't know or need to know.

And I had Lauren and Callie and Glenn and Donna and my new life where I was.

All the sunshine in California couldn't beat that.

dwelling

I slept until one on Saturday and ate cereal in the kitchen. It was very quiet in the house.

I was trying to avoid thinking about the last conversation with Mom. That stuff she said about wasting her life, and being miserable, and trying to make a decent life for us got to me.

It was hard to stop thinking about that, sitting on our worn-out couch, looking at the walls that needed to be painted, so I wandered over to the library. I asked about Janet and her baby. All was well. Margaret said it was so nice to see me and everyone missed me. I took out a bunch of videos. As an afterthought, I took out a few books of poetry. I wasn't going to read the exact stuff Mr. Brody assigned, but I'd read some stuff like it. Anyways, I had already read most of the stuff that was in the poetry book. "The Road Not Taken," and "The Love Song of J. Alfred Prufrock," and all the usual anthology stuff.

I went back home, fell asleep, and woke up about an hour later feeling better.

I decided I should give Lauren a call. A follow-up kind of deal. I brushed my teeth before calling. I got out a pad and started to list things:

1. fun time last night
2. talk about movie, did you like the ending?
3. who do you hang out with at school? do you like them?

The first three items on my list took me over ten minutes to perfect. I decided this was really a pretty bad approach to having a conversation with a girl who was almost getting close to the point where we were approaching a stage that might be called the stage right before the stage of Going Out. We weren't exactly deep into a heavy relationship yet, but the idea wasn't completely impossible to imagine.

And imagination was something I definitely had plenty of. I hung out on the couch and imagined what it would be like to have a real girlfriend. I would wake up in the morning and my first thought would be, like, I can't wait to see her. Then heading to school we would be thinking about each other. We'd hang out a little before first period. Maybe she'd put her hands in my back pockets. We'd see each other in a bunch of classes. We wouldn't make a great big production about being together, but we'd catch each other's eyes and it would be this complete communication from across the room. We'd eat together at lunch. Then after school, we'd hang out. We could be at her house, but I didn't know what her parents were like. If we came to my house, it would be a different story. We'd have the place to ourselves.

This was where things got interesting. We would have the run of the house. We could do whatever we wanted. And what would that be? I could think of a thing or two that I would want to do. But would she be interested in doing the same things I had in mind? I really couldn't tell. I guess I didn't have any sense about her feelings about that stuff.

I called Lauren. Her stepfather answered again.

"Hi. This is Kirk Tobak. May I speak to Lauren?"

"Hello, Kurt. This is her dad. Lauren's not home. She's out with her mother."

"Oh. Okay. Well, if it's okay, if you could just tell her that Kirk called, and I'll try her again."

"Sure thing. You have yourself a good evening, now, Kurt."

"Kirk. Thank you, sir. You, too. Good night."

"Good night, Kurt."

"It's Kirk," I said to the dead line. I dialed Callie's number.

"How are you?" she asked.

"Oh, good. I was just hanging around. And you know, it occurs to me. You really need to pick another book. I think we're going to finish tomorrow."

"I'll think about it. So how was your big date?"

"Oh, it was good. Really good. I think she liked me."

"I'm sure she did. What's not to like?"

"I don't know," I said before I realized it was a rhetorical question.

"So you're just hanging around at home with your Mom?"

"Uh-huh. Right. We're just pretty much doing nothing, really. How about you?"

"I was just on the computer."

"What do you mean?"

"I was on the Internet."

"Um . . . how does that work?"

"I have software that makes everything audio."

"I thought you hate those electronic voices."

"Well, it would be a lot better if it had your stunning voice, but what can I do? It's better than nothing."

"No offense, but you're in pretty bad shape if you like my voice better than the sound of traffic."

"What can I tell you? I'm used to it. I have something on the stove. I'll see you tomorrow?"

"Definitely."

I made spaghetti again. There were still a few meat-balls left in the package and that made for a pretty healthy dinner. I started eating in the kitchen, but it was so quiet that I began to feel like an old man who had nobody left, just shuffling back and forth between rooms and eating his little dinner all by himself. It creeped me out, so I went into the living room and watched a movie while I ate.

I dozed off on the couch when the phone rang. It was Lauren.

"I was out before," she said. "What are you doing?"

"Nothing really. Just kind of hanging around."

"That was a pretty good time last night."

"You liked the movie?"

"That, too," she said. Which had to mean either one of two things: either she meant the pizza, or she meant me. There was no real way to clarify without looking like a total misfit, so I let it go. Knowing that I would agonize over it later.

"Yeah, well, I had a great time, too. The best, really. It was great." Do it. "Going out with you."

"Yeah, well, anyways. I guess I'll see you in school Monday."

"I'll be there."

So all night I replayed the conversation in my mind. If I had it on tape, I could have prepared a transcript and cross-referenced it, but since I didn't, I couldn't do that.

I *could* take notes, though. Which is exactly what I did.

There were a bunch of parts that I had to figure out. The main ones:

One: After I said it was great going out with her, she said, "Yeah, well, anyways." That could definitely be read as some kind of dismissal. Like, "Yeah, right, it was a real thrill." *Anyways* is usually used to change a boring or uncomfortable topic. Which would be me: boring and/or uncomfortable in her eyes. Maybe she felt too uncomfortable with me saying "going out with you." On the other hand, it could be that she got a little shy because she liked me and was nervous about it.

Two: "I guess I'll see you in school on Monday," she said. It was the "I guess" part that was concerning. It wasn't exactly enthusiastic. It wasn't like "Wow, I can't wait to see you in school on Monday," or even "I'm looking forward to seeing you on Monday." As far as I could tell the whole thing about seeing me on Monday was a reference to business as usual; Monday, school, life as usual. In other words, even though we went out, everything is exactly as it was before. It's like we never even went out at all. It also was a pretty strong way of saying that she definitely didn't want to see me or speak to me on Sunday. She'd see me only when she absolutely had to, which would be in school.

Three: My last words, after she said she'd see me in school on Monday: "I'll be there." *I'll be there?* Well, duh. Where else would I be, out working on the assembly line? Of course I'd be there. It was just a bad end to the conversation. It made no impression, it wasn't funny, it wasn't slick, it was nothing. An ending like that had to make her think that I was the most boring kid on the planet. That's what I get for not planning ahead.

This went on in my head until finally even my own mind got sick of it and shut off, hitting the snooze button for the night.

I was walking to the hallway, kind of involved in my thoughts when I heard Glenn call me: "Yo, Hob. What, you just walk by?"

"I was thinking about some stuff. What's up?"

He and a bunch of his friends were hanging around the hall near the back of the school where the smoking section was.

"Where you going?" he asked.

"History."

"Ditch."

"Huh?"

"Cut. Skip. Hang out with us."

Now, as much as I hated most of my classes, I didn't really cut. At heart, I was still kind of a rule-follower that way.

"Well, we have a test coming up. He might review."

"Who cares. You're smart. You'll do fine anyways, if you want to. Besides," he said. He tilted his head to the right. I looked.

Lauren was there, talking to her friends.

"History sucks, anyway," I said. I stood by while Glenn and his friends talked about rock bands that I'd never heard of. I waited to catch Lauren's eye.

A couple of minutes later, she looked up. She smiled at me. She came over.

"Hey," she said.

"Hey. I'm cutting," I said, trying to sound casual, like I did it every day. "Ditching history."

"Yeah?"

"You know what they say. Those who fail history are doomed to repeat it."

She actually laughed. Which helped me get my guts up.

"That was fun, going out, I mean. I mean, I had a good time. I hope you did."

"Yeah, definitely. I told you I did."

"Right, I know. Well, so, what if we do it again?"

"What do you mean, 'what if'?"

"Oh, I'm just saying, maybe we should do stuff together." Well, that sounded great. Stuff could be anything from sex to going on a crime spree. Neither one of which was too appropriate for me to be suggesting at this point in our relationship. Idiot. "Like go out and hang out and you know." There's another good one. Why not just wink at her and wag your eyebrows, Mr. Smooth.

"I'm up for it," she said.

"Great."

That's when she took my hand and held it.

We hung out there, holding hands, cutting class.

Just like a couple.

Callie got a package in the mail and she asked me who it was from.

"It says 'Culinary Finders' and it's from Chicago."

"Oh, great. That's a type of saffron that I've been looking for. Anything else?"

"Bills. And another letter from that Ted Burnham."

"Junk it."

"Who is he?"

"Don't worry about it."

"Well, he seems to want to get in touch with you. Maybe you should just—"

"Look, it's really none of your business, is it?"

Whoa. I looked up. Her eyes were narrowed, maybe closed, and her shoulders were kind of up. Her jaw looked tight.

"Sorry. I didn't mean to get, you know, too personal or anything. I'm sorry."

"No, forget it. My fault. Just do me a favor, and throw it away."

"Absolutely."

We finished *Catch-22*. She didn't laugh that much, but part of that may have been because the ending is really pretty grim. Still, I could tell something was on her mind.

We had a spicy cold soup that she said was gazpacho, and then some kind of chicken stew, which was great. I complimented her on the food, and she nodded and smiled, kind of a weak, fake smile, if you asked me. Callie didn't say a word while we ate, and I was pretty sure it had something to do with me asking probing questions about the letter. I got my coat and she walked me to the door.

"So, I'll see you tomorrow," I said. "Right? You want me to come, right?"

"Of course. Why not?"

"Nothing. Just checking."

She reached out and waved at my arm once before touching it.

"Listen. All it is, Ted was a relationship I had."

"Oh."

"It was actually more than that. We were engaged to be married. Three years ago."

"You were?"

"Yeah. We actually met on a blind date, if you can believe it. I know, it sounds like a bad joke. But we got along so well. He seemed to be totally comfortable with me, in every way. But then as we got closer to the wedding, I started to understand him in a whole different way. And it was pretty awful."

"What was it?"

"Well, it started to be clear to me that it wasn't really that he loved me as much as it was he loved the idea of being able to love me."

"I'm a little lost."

"He liked the idea that he was the kind of guy that could look past the fact that I was blind. It made him feel like he was so open-minded and accepting. When he looked at me, all he saw was how being with me reflected on him. How *he* looked. It actually was sickening."

"I can see that."

She shook her head. "But he was starting to get impatient about a lot of things that were a part of me and my life. Just daily stuff like picking clothes, shopping, not knowing what some actor looks like. I could see that he really wasn't going to be able to handle it in the long haul. He was getting snappy with me, and sooner or later, he was going to resent me."

"That's pretty rotten."

She nodded and was quiet for a few seconds.

"Then what?" I asked.

"Well, then he started talking to some old girlfriend. He said she called him first, but I knew where *that* was heading. I broke the engagement and dumped him."

"Good."

"Hey. I may be blind, but I'm not blind."

"Oh. I'm sorry about all that." I didn't know what you're supposed to say to things like that.

"Now he's trying to make up." She shook her head. She sighed. "So that's my sorry little story. Sorry to dump it on you. It just gets me upset. It was a pretty rough time. A lot of heartache. I thought I had put it all behind me and then this letter comes, which brought back some of that heartache. I guess it's still a bit of a raw spot for me. I try, I've worked really hard not to dwell on things that are over and done with. But sometimes it just comes back and it's hard to get rid of."

I was actually pretty surprised that she would tell me those things. We never really talked much about personal stuff, but there she was, trusting me.

"Look," she said. "I'm really sorry I snapped at you before. It's not your fault at all."

I reached out to touch her arm, but I realized that would be sort of weird. It was a little physical, really, and I was afraid it might be kind of inappropriate or something. I just kind of brushed my hand up into my hair.

"No problem at all," I said.

"I'm glad I can really talk to you."

"Me, too."

Glenn was upstairs getting drinks. He was frustrated with a twelve-bar song that kept becoming an eight-bar song, whatever that meant. I was alone with Donna. She was standing, bent over at the waist. Her hair fell straight to the floor.

"Back's bad?" I asked.

"Sucks," she said.

"When did you have the operation?"

"Summer before sophomore year. I had to sit out the whole year."

"Were you scared before the operation?"

"It was pretty bad. I was almost willing to skip the whole thing, but they wouldn't let me. They said it would get worse. It's like, which pain do I want?"

"Horrible pain, or miserable pain."

"Exactly. You got it."

"So which did you end up getting?"

"Horrible *and* miserable pain."

"Two for the price of one," I said.

"Yeah. Lucky me."

"Well, it looks like it worked out for the best," I said.

"Yeah, well, I still have pain. But I guess pain is part of life."

"I guess."

We were quiet for a while. I didn't really know what to say.

"So, sounds like Lauren is pretty hot for you."

"What?"

"She likes you."

"What did she say?"

"She says she likes you."

"She said that? What else?"

"Nothing. That you're pretty intense."

"What does she mean by that?"

"Well you are." She turned to Glenn. "Isn't he?"

"What?" Glenn said. He handed a beer to Donna. He gave me a Pepsi.

"Lauren's saying I'm intense. Does she mean that in a good way?"

"I guess. She likes you. She's pretty intense, too."

"Perfect match," Glenn said.

I looked at him. "Hold on. Was this whole thing a set-up?"

"Of course. We knew you'd be perfect together."

I didn't even know what to say to that. "What else can you tell me about her?"

"What do you wanna know?" Donna asked. She took a big swig of her beer. It foamed up a little.

"Tell me about her past boyfriends."

"Forget it. Ask her."

"Well, give me a hint."

"Nope. You wanna know that stuff, you ask her."

"You're not helping."

"What do you want me to say? She slept with practically every guy in the school and a bunch of the girls, too."

"What?" My heart just about stopped. "Is that true?"

"No, actually she took a vow of chastity. She's gonna be a nun," Glenn said.

They were driving me crazy.

"I'd say it's somewhere in between," Donna said.

"Come on. Well, closer to which end?" Donna gave me a look. "You're jerking me around because I'm being a jerk. Right?"

"Totally. Just relax and see where things go with her."

That seemed like pretty good advice. But again, easier to say than to do.

Glenn was working a little five-note part over and over again, changing the fourth and fifth notes to try to find something he liked. I was trying to work out a phrase in a new thing I was writing, and I couldn't concentrate with him playing that same thing again and again. I looked up at him to see if he was fooling around, doing it to drive me crazy. But he wasn't, he was staring down at the strings, digging into the notes.

~~A blast of scars~~
~~A constellation of scars~~

"Are you almost done with that part?" I asked him.

"I can't get it." He tried another combination, which sounded awful to me. "I think that's it," he said.

"That didn't sound right."

"That's a basic blues turnaround."

"Maybe, but I'm just saying. It sounded off to me."

"You stick to the words. I know what I'm doing." Then he played the whole part before, and when he came to the bit that I didn't like, it sounded much better.

"You're right," I said. He shrugged and played the whole thing over again.

I turned back to the part I was working on.

A starburst of scars glow in the night
Nothing to say, my voice is shot
A lone gunman, with nothing in sight

Glenn was playing the new part again, and now it sounded really good to me. "How come you're still doing this alone?" I asked him.

"Doing what?" He put down his guitar pick and took a chug of his beer.

"Playing by yourself. Why don't you get in a band or something?"

"What for?"

"So you can share your musical genius with the awaiting public. I mean, what kind of world would this be if Liberace had kept his talent all to himself?"

"That's a really flattering comparison. Thanks."

"What do you think, Donna?"

"I keep telling him." Donna was stretched out on the BarcaLounger, trying to sleep.

"Seriously. Wouldn't it be pretty cool to actually get on a stage with some other people and play live? Don't tell me you haven't thought about it."

"Sometimes."

"So do it. Seize the day, son," I said.

"Who you calling 'son,' son? I got *sperm* bigger than you."

Callie wanted to read Raymond Carver stories. I had heard of him, but never got around to reading him. I was looking forward to it.

She seemed to be in a better mood during the week. I figured she had gotten over the bad feelings she had about that guy. I was kind of curious about that whole part of Callie, her being in a relationship and all.

When I got there on Thursday, Callie was in kind of a nervous mood.

"Come into the kitchen. I need a hand." I took off my coat and followed her. She had her plastic containers of food lined up on all of the counters and the table. There were four big insulated plastic coolers on the floor.

"I have a pickup in ten minutes, and some of this is going to a new place and I got behind schedule and I think I got a whole bunch of these mixed up. I don't have time to open each container and get it all sorted out. Listen. There should be seven different types of food here. A soup that's red, a stew that's probably a little more brown, a light colored soup, a green soup, a white stew, a blackish purple bean dip, and something that looks like cubed vegetables in a broth."

"Okay. I can count six, no seven, different types of stuff."

"Good. I need five of each in each of these containers."

"Wow. Okay."

"What's this?" she asked, holding up a container.

"It's the green thing. Just, you know what? It might be kind of faster if I do all of it myself."

"Really. Okay. I'm sorry, we're a little pressed for time."

I started by counting off five of each thing and putting them in batches. Then I moved them to the coolers. "Where does all of this go?"

"To different gourmet food shops in the area. I'm starting with a new one and I want to make sure everything is right. I like to have everything ready for Michael when he gets here."

"No problem. Relax. I'm sure this Michael will wait if we're not done."

"Well, I don't want him to wait. I want it all ready."

"Okay, it will be. But, I mean, I can't believe they wouldn't understand if you had a little problem being exactly on time. I mean, it sounds like Michael is your regular pick-up guy? Doesn't he know you're blind?"

"Yes, he knows, but I just like to have everything right, okay? Let's just get it done, please."

"You got it."

Lauren said she had to go to her grandmother's in Pennsylvania for the weekend, but she could spend a little time with me after school on Friday. We stood in front of the school trying to decide where to go. Glenn saw me and started heading my way. When he saw that I was standing with Lauren, he stopped, gave me a thumbs-up and headed to his car.

We couldn't really come up with anyplace to go except our houses.

"My little brother is going to be practicing his trumpet and I can't take it," she said. "How about your house?"

I had a ridiculous thought that this was the beginning of a letter to the editor of a porno magazine. Not too likely, but my place sounded just fine.

"Hang on one second," I told her, squeezing through the door. I wanted to make sure the place was presentable, that I didn't leave laundry on the living room floor or anything. The coast was more or less clear. Nothing horrifying, anyway.

"Come on in."

I kind of avoided the house tour for pretty obvious

reasons. I got her settled in the living room. I put on the radio.

"So, let me get something for you to drink. So, what, soda okay? Or something hot? I don't really have any beer or anything like that."

"Anything's okay."

I went into the kitchen. I tried to calm down.

I kind of tried to imagine how Glenn would act, how he would talk, how he would be so cool and relaxed. It would probably be cool to make coffee, but since I never drank it myself, I really didn't know how to make it. I'd have to start drinking it sometime soon. I thought of making tea, but I had this idea that if I left her for too long, she'd come to her senses and bolt. I poured soda. Kid stuff, I know, but at least it was safe. I brought the drinks back to the living room.

She took it.

"So this is it. Not exactly Shangri-La, but we call it home. So. Here we are. Of course. That's really such a dopey statement, 'Here we are.' Where else would we be?"

She laughed.

"You know what's another stupid expression? 'I could care less.' People don't get it, they have it backward. If you could care less about something, then that really means the thing you're talking about isn't at the very bottom of your caring totem pole. If you say 'I couldn't care less,' you mean there's nothing at all that you could care less about than the thing you're talking about. So, I'm just rambling like a total lunatic. Feel free to fall asleep or punch me in the mouth to shut me up."

"I like when you talk."

"Well, we'll have to get you some professional help."

She laughed, and shivered. "Why is it so cold in here?"

"Oh, well, see we have the heat turned down. My mom is kind of funny that way. Saving money, or something. Crazy. You're that cold?"

"Well, yeah. It's kind of freezing in here."

"It's warmer upstairs." Oh, man. Mr. Subtlety, starring Kirk Tobak. "I mean, it is. Really, because heat rises? And so that's why it's warmer up there."

"Okay, let's go up."

It was almost inconceivable: There was a girl in my bedroom. Even Ripley's Believe It or Not! would say, "Come on, you think we'll fall for just anything?"

"So where is your Mom, anyway?" she asked. "At work?"

"She went on a little trip. She does that. She won't be home anytime soon." I worried for a second that it sounded like I was saying that we'd be alone for a long time, so, *ma chérie* . . .

"Yeah, I know that deal. My mom isn't around too much, either."

"Where is she?"

"Anywhere but home, if she can help it," Lauren said. She was looking at the Arbus photo of the strange Brooklyn family. "She pretty much regrets having me and my brother. She had us kind of young and she really doesn't much like us."

"Maybe she's unhappy about other stuff."

"Definitely, that too. She's basically a pretty unhappy

person and part of that is to make everyone else around her unhappy I guess. Maybe that's why my father took off when I was like eight."

"Really? Mine left when I was a baby."

"That totally sucks. Do you hate him?"

"Well, I never even really got to know him. It's kind of hard to hate someone you don't remember at all. I just never had a father, so I didn't really know what I was missing."

"Still. That's so shitty." She sighed and walked slowly around my room. Somehow I believed that she was thinking how we had some things in common. Maybe I thought she was thinking that just because it's what I was thinking myself.

"No lie," she said. "I was pretty pissed when my father left. He just took off one night after another big blowout fight. No visits, just Christmas cards. Asshole."

Her lips set and kind of went tight and I could see the muscles in her jaw moving. I didn't know what I was supposed to do. It sounds like a cliché, but I felt like there was some kind of new connection that hadn't been there five minutes earlier. Or maybe it had been there and we just didn't know it. I wondered if I should touch her arm or hold her hand or something. She moved closer to the picture. "What a fucked-up family."

"What, yours or the one in the picture?"

"Both."

"Well, you know what Tolstoy said. 'Happy families are all alike. But fucked-up families are fucked-up in their own ways.'"

She laughed. "Tolstoy said that?"

"Kind of. He said it in Russian, so that's sort of a modern and weird translation."

She sat down on the bed next to me. She looked at me. She was looking right in my eyes. I tried to make sure that she couldn't hear my breathing.

She was sitting on my bed, and this was it. I leaned in and kissed her. She kissed me back. After a minute or two, she pulled back. I half expected her to leap out the window. But she didn't.

I held my breath.

"Relax," she said.

She knew what she was doing. Not that I had anyone to compare to, but I knew for sure that Lauren really knew how to kiss. And while we kissed, she put her hands on the back of my head, and put her fingers in my hair. That was so nice, I felt my heart pound. I kept my hands on her back, resisting the urge to move them around to her front. This was good, and I didn't want to push it, to ruin it.

It was good to just be happy.

That night, I was feeling great, in bed and in that really relaxing feeling just before floating into sleep, and then the phone rang. I tried to ignore it so it wouldn't ruin my good feeling. Just before the machine clicked on, the ringing stopped. Then it started again. I jumped up and ran into Mom's room, figuring that it might be Lauren.

I turned on the light and grabbed the phone.

It was Mom. I couldn't tell if she was drunk, or just really emotional. But as she talked, I started to feel light-headed. I grabbed onto her headboard, dizzy, because it felt like the floor was swelling up like a stormy sea.

frayed

Every summer a traveling carnival would set up in a field that was just outside of town. Kids rode their bikes over and watched as the carnies set up the usual rides: the Octopus, the Whip, plus half-size Ferris wheels and roller coasters. There was sawdust and straw all over the field, crappy arcade games where balls were thrown at holes just a tiny bit too small. There was a petting zoo with stinky goats and mangy sheep. Food vendors sold grilled sausage and peppers, lemonade, and cotton candy. As cheesy as it was, it was always packed once it opened, and I loved being in all the lights and sounds and excitement.

I must have been around eight when I went with Mom and they had a ride they'd never had before. It was called the Tilt-a-Whirl. It looked huge to me, a big ring where the riders stood up facing the center, their backs against red padded cushions. The whole point of the ride was an exercise in centrifugal force, but I wasn't thinking of that at the time. I was thinking about what would happen if the spinning drum spun off. Would it fly off into space, or would it roll over the petting zoo and the cars in the parking lot?

Mom took my hand and pulled me into the line snaking around the gray metal barricades. We got in adjoining cages. The tattooed worker strapped a very worn harness across my chest. The straps were frayed on the edges and, rather than making me feel safe, it made me wonder what other parts of the ride were frayed and worn.

Mom grinned at me as we started to spin. As we picked up speed, I felt my guts pressing into the back of my body and my body pressing into the red cushion. The wheel spun faster and faster. The fairgrounds, the whole world became a big multicolored blur.

Then the wheel started to tilt higher and higher. As if it wasn't bad enough before, now we were spinning toward the earth, away from the earth, toward, away, until I lost my sense of what was up and what was down. Everything was crazy, alien. I was disoriented and terrified.

And that was when the floor beneath my feet dropped away.

"Hey, baby," Mom was saying from California. "We just got in and, even though it's late over there, I wanted to call you right away. Things are going so good here, the restaurant deal looks like it's going to happen, but the reason I called is to tell you something. Guess what? Hal and I just got back from Las Vegas where you won't believe what happened. We got married!"

That was the part where I got dizzy and had to find something to hold me up.

"Honey? Are you there? Did you hear what I said?"

"Uh-huh. Married."

"Yes! Of course, we would have wanted you to be there, but we just kind of got swept away by the whole wedding chapel thing and all the excitement."

"You got married," I repeated like some kind of moron.

"It's so exciting, I can't believe it! We're really going to be a family."

I didn't say anything. If the fate of Western Civilization depended on it, I couldn't have found words.

She lowered her voice to something like a stage whisper. "Listen. I know you have some issues about Hal, even though I don't really understand what that's all about. But we're going to have such a great life. It's all going to be different."

"Mm."

"We're going to live out here and we can work together. You can work at the restaurant with us. It's going to be so great!"

The conversation had taken a totally surreal turn. It was like two other people talking about totally other lives.

"I can't talk now. There's something . . ."

"Something what?"

"I don't know. On the stove. I have to hang up now."

"Honey?"

I hung up the phone.

I grabbed the first thing I could reach and threw it across the room. But it was just a pillow and it plopped pathetically on the floor by the door. It made me feel worse. I grabbed the lamp on her night table and I was set to hurl it at the mirror over her old, scarred dresser.

But I felt ridiculous. It was too much like a bad TV-movie scene, to shatter a mirror with a lamp. I knew I'd feel even worse if I did it, cheap and clichéd. I dropped the lamp on the bed and sat on the floor. My head was spinning and I remembered what I felt like as a kid in the Tilt-a-Whirl.

I was up most of the night, just tossing and turning in my bed, stuck awake. I couldn't seem to get rid of the grotesque image of Mom and Hal in a pink and red Chapel of Love, saying their vows for an Elvis impersonator.

I woke up late and still couldn't clear my head of the depressing thoughts. They really would try to move to California. Would I actually have to live in the same house with Hal? Did they think I would do it? Did they think I would call him *Dad*?

I was pacing around the living room, back and forth, murmuring to myself, "I can't believe it. I can't believe it," like a deranged person. My nerves were frayed.

I was worried that I was becoming unhinged, and I had to get some kind of grip.

Later, I was on my back in bed and I could actually think straight for the first time in about twenty-four hours. I didn't know how it would all turn out, but I wasn't going to roll over and give up without a fight. I wasn't about to go out to live in California and I wasn't planning on having a father-son game of catch with Hal in the backyard. I was just going to go on with my life, which had finally started working out for me. I just had to make sure that nobody found out. I figured that technically, Mom could probably be charged with abandonment. But if anyone told the people at school, the obvious thing would be to get Mom back home or to ship me out to California. Thank you, no.

I had to make sure that nobody found out. And I had to just go on with my life like nothing was different, like my whole damned future wasn't about to become a complete and total train wreck.

running water

It didn't take Glenn a lot of work to convince me to cut Spanish, not when I saw Lauren hanging around with them. I got a cut slip for ditching History, and I forged my mom's signature, like all the cutters did. This would be number two, and three would mean detention.

I said hi to Lauren.

"Hi," she said, one eyebrow raised. She was really pretty cute. She came toward me and I leaned in to kiss her.

"How was your grandmother's?" I asked.

"Oh, a thrill a minute. I thought about you a lot."

"Me? Really?"

"Yeah. A lot. What did you do?"

Ah. Somehow I knew, there were a million wrong answers to that question and one right answer. And I knew what the right answer was. "I thought about you."

"Really?"

"Really." It was true, of course. I was thinking about Lauren a lot.

"You know, you're a good kisser," she whispered in my ear.

Me? Was she talking about *me*? "Well, you're a *great* kisser."

"So I guess we make a pretty good couple."

She hooked her thumbs in my belt loops and pulled me up against her.

Screw classes. Detention wouldn't bother me. I could get used to this.

I was going pretty much out of my mind that night, having totally different feelings. Even though I was just about 110 percent sure that Mom's unholy union with Hal would fizzle out, the whole thing was still disturbing and disgusting enough to make me edgy. Even the thought of having to live with him made me feel sick. And then, on the other hand, things were going great with Lauren, better than I could have imagined even a month before. I had the bad stuff in California and great stuff at home happening to me all at once. Total extremes.

I finished reading the book of Raymond Carver stories with Callie. What I really liked about them was the way they seemed simple, and yet how there always seemed to be so much more going on under the surface of things. It's like everyone always has their own story, their own private world.

We were having a hard time deciding what to read

next. We went into the kitchen, where she served me some chili.

"Wow. What did you put in here, plutonium?"

"Too hot?"

"No, it's good. Taste buds grow back, right?"

"I don't know. We'll see. The body is an amazing thing."

I looked at her. Somehow, her comment hit me kind of hard. With her vision problem and all, and the scars around her eyes, this was a pretty powerful thing for her to say.

"Callie?" I decided to ask. "What happened?"

She nodded slowly, twice. "You've been wondering for a long time and couldn't figure out how to ask."

"Kind of."

"Well, you picked the right way. It was ten years ago. I had just turned eighteen. My parents took me out to dinner at this really fancy place, the absolute best food, about forty minutes from where we lived. We were heading home. My father was driving, I was next to him, my mother dozing off in the back seat. Basically a car crossed into our lane. Head-on."

She cleared her throat.

"The crash would have been bad no matter what, but the thing was, there was a defect in our car. The two front seats tore away. My father and I went through the wind-shield. He died instantly. My mother died in the back seat. Somehow, I made it out in one piece. Pretty much."

There wasn't a thing in the world I could think of to say.

Callie shrugged. "That's what happened."

"I've never heard of anything like that. It's like a miracle you lived. If the seat hadn't ripped out, your father might have lived? You'd be able to see?"

"Who knows? The seats coming out sure didn't help. We sued the hell out of the car company. I'm pretty well-set."

"Oh. So the cooking business. You don't have to do it for the money?"

"It's just for fun. Like I say, I'm pretty well-set."

I sat there for a minute, mulling all of it over in my head. I had kind of suspected it had been something horrible, but I just didn't really imagine it as this awful.

"You know," I said. "It's amazing how you can just tell that whole horrible story and it doesn't shake you up, like, to talk about it."

"It was a long time ago."

"Still. I mean I'd think a person would just be crazy with, you know, rage, or sadness or frustration, or something. I don't know."

"I did all that. Look, remember when I asked you if you were mad about your dad leaving you when you were a kid? Remember what you said?"

"This is different, though."

"Yes and no. You said, 'It's just part of my life. There's really nothing to be mad about. It's the way it is.' You can be mad and live your life being pissed off, or you can move on. It's really not different."

She got up and went to the counter, where she tore off two more chunks of bread. She sat back down and handed me a hunk.

"Look at it this way. What religion are you?"

"Oh, man. I think there were a few religions in our

family, so they pretty much cancel each other out. I'm kind of nothing."

"Okay, well, I'm a lapsed Catholic. But a few years after this, I started looking into Eastern religions like Buddhism and Taoism. A lot of it makes sense, you know? A lot of them are really about going with the flow. There is suffering in life, it's a fact. People run into trouble when they can't accept that suffering and pain is going to happen anyway, so accept it as part of life and move on. Go with the flow."

"So it's that simple?"

"Well, I'm oversimplifying it, but still, the idea is simple. I agree it's not that simple to feel it. But over time I came to understand how much sense it makes. There's this great analogy about the reflection of the moon on a river. The water runs, it keeps moving, but the moonlight's reflection is always there. You know? Stuff happens, but in the end, you're still there. You always have yourself."

"What if you don't want to have yourself?" I asked.

"Well, then that's something else you have to deal with. You're stuck with yourself for life."

"By definition."

"Exactly. You ever hear the expression, 'No matter where you go, there you are'? Every time you turn around, you're still going to be there. Might as well learn to like the company. So get used to it. You have to learn to deal with it, is what I'm saying."

I looked at Callie. I had never met anybody like her.

Glenn wanted to go get some CDs. I was pretty quiet in the car, looking out at the gray, wasted strip malls. It wasn't exactly what anybody would call scenic, but still. It was home for me. And the alternative was much more depressing to me than the dirty snow that lined the edges of the highway.

"What's with you?" Glenn asked.

"What?"

"You're quiet."

I shrugged. I thought about telling him, but I didn't want to get into the whole thing. It was possible that Glenn might think the idea of moving to California sounded cool, and I didn't want to debate it, or explain about Mom, or Hal, or any of that. I just didn't even want to talk about it at all. And more important, even though I pretty much trusted him, I couldn't take a chance that he might accidentally tell someone and I could get into trouble about living alone. I'd have to keep it to myself.

I didn't have money to spend on CDs, so I wandered around the store and stopped at a bulletin board. I looked at all the cards and notices tacked up: used instruments, used CDs, amplifiers. One of them was kind of interesting to me. I went over to Glenn.

"What's an 'ax'?" I asked him.

"You're the genius. You tell me."

"It's a guitar, right?"

"See? I knew you were smart."

"So an 'ax-man' is a guitarist."

"Amazing. Just brilliant."

We got to his house and went down to the basement. He

put one of his new CDs in his player and flicked on his amp. I went upstairs and took out the strip of paper I had torn off one of the notices in the store. I dialed the number and got an answering machine. I cleared my throat and lowered my voice a little bit.

"Hi, I'm calling about your notice about a classic rock ax-man. My name is Glenn Scharff. Gimme a call and we'll set something up." I left Glenn's number and hung up.

One day, we went to Lauren's house after school. Her brother was in the basement playing video games, and both of her parents were out.

We ended up in her bedroom. I don't know what I expected, but it was different from what I imagined it would be. It was just kind of basic. Light green walls, no posters or anything, basic furniture. The top of her dresser was covered with about fifty tiny bottles of makeup and perfumes and stuff like that. She kind of wore makeup around her eyes, eyeliner, I guess, but I never really pictured her putting it on. It was like seeing into a private side of her that I knew must have existed, but couldn't exactly picture.

She put the radio on. She pulled the bottom drawer completely out of her dresser and took out a small wooden box from somewhere inside the dresser. She sat on her bed, Indian style, and opened the box.

"So you don't party, huh?" she asked.

"Not really."

"Just don't want to?"

"There are substance issues in my family."

"Oh. Well, I'm going to, if it won't bother you."

"Go ahead." She started rolling her joint.

I wandered around the room, as if there were something to look at, while she smoked her joint. "Is it my imagination, or does the wall look totally different right here?" I said. I rubbed my hand on a two-foot square patch that was smoother than the rest of the wall.

"No, it's different. I kind of threw a bowling ball through that wall."

"You what?"

"It's a long story. We've had some 'issues' of our own. Or I did. 'Anger management' issues. 'Low tolerance for frustration' was another one. I was pretty big into throwing stuff."

"Like bowling balls."

"Among other things."

I sat down next to her. "What was it about?"

"Mainly about when my father left. I was just totally pissed off at him, at the world, at everything. He took off and I got really angry. And then my mother came down on me and turned into this total bitch, saying that I was making her wrecked life even worse, without even caring about what I was going through. She was just embarrassed or whatever that her husband left her. So she turned all her angry shit on me, and I was pretty much fucked by both of them."

"So what happened?"

"I was able to figure out a whole different approach. I'm not gonna sit back and take shit from life. The hell with that. Life can take shit from me. My turn, now. Like, live for today. Do what I want. I'm young and I'm just gonna feel good and have fun."

"Sounds good," I said.

She blew smoke onto the end of her joint, which glowed orange. She looked at it and smiled. "Do you have any idea what I'm talking about?"

"What, you mean like feeling totally betrayed, left alone, and deciding to take care of yourself? No idea at all."

She smiled and pinched out the stub of the joint.

"How did you get put in our English class?" she asked. "You're too smart for it."

"Believe me, I'm not so smart."

"I think you are."

"You must be mistaking me for someone else."

"You get stuff. It's in your writing. You know? It's like so much stuff I think about myself. How everyone is just superficial. Not Glenn and Donna, but pretty much every-one else. It's like nobody has any feelings, really. They're just total androids. You know what I'm talking about?"

"I know exactly what you're talking about."

"I know you do. I don't know. I just . . . It seems like there aren't too many people like me, like who I can relate to. Do you ever feel like you're just totally different?"

She looked me in the eyes. I looked into hers and I felt this total connection, this kindred spirit kind of thing.

"Do you ever feel alone even when you're with other people? Do you know what I mean?"

"Yeah. I know exactly what you mean." I didn't know anyone else who felt that way. "Do you feel alone now?" I asked her.

"No. Not now." She turned to me.

We kissed for a while. I recalled Callie's words, "Go with the flow," and decided to ease up and go when it felt right. After a little while, she moved closer to me and sort of pushed her chest against mine. I went with the flow. It seemed right and she didn't tell me otherwise.

Our breathing started getting pretty heavy and before I knew it, she was pulling her shirt off. I saw she had a tattoo of some kind of Asian word on the back of her shoulder. Her skin was smooth, velvety. She smelled clean, like soap and roses.

She reached down and unsnapped her jeans. The sound of her zipper going down. I couldn't believe this was happening. She took my hand and guided it down.

I realized I was holding my breath and I let it out when my fingertips touched her. She held my hand tightly and moved it. I was going into sensory overload. The word "pink" somehow kept repeating in my mind.

She gripped my hand tightly, holding it with her hand and her thighs squeezed tightly around it. Her breath came in short, deep pants.

She ground against my fingers and her other hand ripped at the snap of my jeans, kind of frantically yanking at the zipper as she moved harder and faster against my hand.

I bit my lip and she took hold of me.

I lost it.

I wanted to cry.

She still held me with her hand. She gripped my hand like a vise between her thighs, squeezing, pushing. She suddenly jerked and arched her hips so hard I worried my wrist might break.

She slowly eased back, her body going slack. "God," she breathed.

"You okay?" I asked.

She laughed. "I'd say I'm okay, yeah." She touched my cheek with the backs of her fingers.

I was pretty embarrassed about losing it so fast, but I was so turned on by her that I just couldn't help it. I wondered what she thought, but I didn't want to bring attention to it.

"You're so good," she said. I wasn't exactly sure what she meant.

But as long as she thought I was good at all, that was good enough.

It was pretty cold in my house. Mom usually kept the house kind of cool, to save money. I was walking around in a T-shirt, shirt, sweatshirt, and a denim jacket. It was pretty uncomfortable. It got colder at night. In my bedroom, I was huddled up in my clothes, under the covers, watching a movie.

The phone rang and I went into Mom's room. I let the machine pick up, and screened. Mom's voice came over the machine: "Hi! It's me! The newlywed, calling for the world's most rotten teenager! Just kidding. Pick up, if you're there!"

Fat chance.

"Hey, come on, don't keep a blushing bride waiting. I wanted to give you an update on married life and life in the fast lane in Los Angeles!" She pronounced the last two words in this bad Spanish accent, and her whole giddy tone somehow made me really mad. I couldn't stand to hear her voice.

"Come on. Pick up! Pick up! I want you to say hi to Hal and congratulate him on getting to marry such an attractive and exciting—"

I didn't hear the next word, because I smashed the answering machine with my fist. It went dead immediately.

It felt good.

Back in bed, I thought about what Lauren had said about being angry and all that. I could totally relate to why she smashed a bowling ball through her wall. If I had one, I probably would have done the same thing.

But I had also been thinking a lot about the things Callie had told me. She had a pretty great way to think about things: things happen, can't stop nature, roll with the punches. It sounded like it made sense, but it seemed a lot harder to do than Lauren's way.

I rubbed my hands together to warm them up, and I decided this was crazy. I turned the thermostat up enough for it to be tolerable.

By morning it was better. In fact it got so comfortable that I slept a little too late. So I had to rush to get dressed and eat. I finished the dishes pretty fast and turned the water off. I was about to leave the kitchen when I noticed a soft hissing sound. I walked around the kitchen, trying to find the source. It got louder near the sink, but the faucet was off. I stood there for a second and then crouched down to open the cabinet beneath the sink. There was a pipe there that was spraying hot water. The buckets and cleaning things were swimming in the couple of inches of water filling the bottom of the cabinet.

I got my hand around the spraying part. The water just sprayed out between my fingers. I held tighter.

Now I don't think there's an animal on the earth that's so stupid that it won't pull back when something hurts it. I'm not sure, but I think even one-celled organisms have reflexes against something uncomfortable. But there I was, gripping a burning hot pipe with my hand. It actually took a few seconds before the pain registered. I yanked my hand back, and smashed my elbow on the inside of the cabinet. It felt like I got shot in the funny bone. My arm burned and buzzed.

Kicking in the cabinet door, of course, didn't much help the pain. And it didn't exactly solve the pipe problem, for that matter. My cursing didn't do much to help either.

I took a look at the leak. It seemed to be coming from a joint between two pipes. It was just a little bit misaligned, I figured. All it needed was to be straightened. I grabbed a dishrag, took hold of the pipe and tried to push it back a little bit.

The spray got much worse.

I wrapped the rag tightly around the leak. The cloth then got precisely as hot as the scalding water. I couldn't hold onto it anymore.

I could see a valve kind of thing and I was brilliant enough to figure a valve was probably some kind of shut-off device. I turned the valve and the water stopped flowing.

I was soaked. But at least it was off. I was going to

have to get a plumber to fix the pipe. I was definitely going to be late for school. I was going to have to deal with a late note from home—which of course I'd have to forge, another slight risk—if I didn't get to school sometime during first period. I ran upstairs and changed my clothes. As I was yanking on my shirt, it occurred to me that I had a vague memory of hearing somewhere that you can't leave pipes off in the winter. If I remembered right, if you didn't have water flowing, just a couple of drops, even, the pipes would freeze. I couldn't remember if that was right or not, or how long it would take pipes to freeze. I put on the news and it was thirty-one degrees out, which meant below freezing.

I got a heavy yellow rubber glove, the cleaning kind, from under the sink. I stretched it and wrapped it super-tight around the leaky joint. I used the other rubber glove to tie the first one onto the pipe. I turned the valve a little bit. There was a groaning sound in the pipes. But the glove didn't leak. Then there was the tiniest trickle, so I twisted the glove a little bit and the trickle stopped.

I got to school halfway through first period. I walked into Physics and said "sorry" to Mr. Chapelle as I took my seat.

"So nice of you to join us," he said.

"Thanks. It's a real pleasure to be here," I answered. He looked like he was going to say something to me, but he turned back to the board and continued reviewing some formulas or something.

Well, I had averted my first little disaster. I was going to have to call a plumber, though. I didn't want to run out of money and let Mom know that I couldn't handle things on my own. I wanted to be totally self-sufficient. But it was pretty clear I'd have to get a professional in when there was a danger of the house flooding and floating down the street.

"Let's put the books away. Time for the quiz I promised you. Last one before the holiday break."

I cleared my desk. My right hand was hurting like crazy. I looked at it. The palm was bright red and had some nasty blisters forming. It burned like mad.

The kid in front of me handed me the test. I picked up my pen, but I couldn't grip it. Not that I knew the material anyway. Still, I had trouble writing my name. I gave up.

I started to imagine that the rubber glove might have popped off the pipe and as I sat there in school, the kitchen was filling up with water. Here was a physics problem that really mattered: how much water could sit on a kitchen floor before it buckled, caving into the crawl space and leaving a jagged crater where the floor used to be? Part B of the problem was to solve for exactly how much money it would cost to replace a kitchen floor. Part C was to calculate the time it would take for the damage from the missing floor to weaken the whole structural framework of the house enough to cause a complete cave-in. Part D was to come up with an explanation to the police.

"What's the problem, Kirk? You need to take this test."

"I can't write."

"Can't, or won't? Let me guess. You have a genetic condition which prevents you from writing on Tuesdays? Or maybe you have more important things to do than study for our test."

Maybe I do, but what would you care? All you people care about is your little subjects. God almighty, who gives a damn about this stuff? What kind of a loser geek can get all excited about this? Well, maybe you do, maybe you get off on all these nice little formulas and neat little laws and everything always works out just the way you predict. But don't inflict this crap on me and expect me to give a damn. I have a life, too, or at least I'm trying to. And I've got problems, bigger problems than this stupid test. If this guy said one more word to me, I knew I might say something inappropriate.

"Are you planning to take the test or are you going to accept the consequences?"

"No, I'm not taking your damned test and you can take me out and shoot me for all I care. I don't give a flying fuck."

The principal's first words to me were, "We need to have a meeting with your mother."

So much for going with the flow.

break

The only way to escape from this one was going to require an act of diversion, distraction, daring, and pure boldness that would make Houdini jealous. Horwich's secretary was getting my contact card, and he was going to call Mom's place of work to set up an appointment. If he got through, he'd find out that I was staying by myself, and I could end up on the California Express.

My hand was burning, but I tried to ignore the pain and come up with a plan before Mr. Horwich made the call. He was a pretty heavyset guy with folds in his neck that covered the collar of his shirt.

"Let's get this settled," he said. This was going to be a problem. This was what I was worried about happening. I had to keep him from calling. And I had no plan. Nothing.

He reached for the phone.

"Mr. Horwich. Could you do me a favor and let me talk

to her first? I can break this to her gently. She's been under a lot of stress at work, and it might help."

"Well, that would be fine."

I pulled the phone toward me and dialed.

"Thank you. I appreciate your understanding."

He smiled.

"Psychic Buddies Hotline, please hold for our next available Psychic."

"Hi," I said. "Is Patty Tobak in? This is her son, Kirk. Thanks. . . . " I tapped my finger for a moment. "Hi, Mom. It's Kirk."

"Hello, I'm your psychic buddy, Fran. Who's this?"

"I'd think you could guess," I said. "I'm at school. No, nothing's wrong."

"I'm glad to hear that. Are you over eighteen?"

"Well, nothing big. I just got in a little trouble at school. Wait, don't yell."

"If you're not eighteen, you can't be doing this without a parent."

"I know you have a big trial coming up, I know it's a big case, but . . . " I shook my head at Horwich, like I was enduring a big lecture. He put out his hand for the phone. I held up my hand.

"Mom? Would you . . . can I get one word in? Mr. Horwich, the principal, wants to talk to you."

"I think you got the wrong number, son," my psychic buddy said, and she hung up. I held the phone tight against my ear in case the disconnection made that loud beeping sound.

"Listen, he needs to talk to you. No. Hold on. Don't

hang up. . . . We can't deal with it at home. He wants to talk to you."

"Let me talk to her, Kirk."

I stood up and raised my voice into the phone.

"I cursed in class. I don't know, I lost my temper about something. Yes, it's wrong. Of course I will, if he'll accept an apology. I know you have stuff going on, and I'm sorry. If it were up to me, I wouldn't have bothered you before a trial, but he needs to talk to you."

"I'll talk to her," Mr. Horwich said.

"I'm handing over the phone, Mom. You have to talk to him, now. No, I'm putting him on. Don't hang up."

I held the receiver against my chest and whispered to Horwich, "She's kind of edgy. She's under a lot of pressure."

I handed the phone to Mr. Horwich. "Mrs. Tobak?" He listened for a moment. "Nobody there," he said to me.

Just then, I heard the piercing warning to say we were disconnected.

Mr. Horwich put down the phone.

"Sorry about that," I said. I looked down. "I'm a little embarrassed."

"I understand. Why don't you just go on back to class."

"Okay."

And I'd also like to thank the Members of the Academy. . . .

"Where were you?" Glenn asked when I got to English late.

"Long story," I said.

"Well, here come your finals for *Of Mice and Men*." Mr. Brody began to move through the room handing back the final exams, facedown. "Anybody know the word *euthanasia*?" Of course, nobody seemed to know the word for mercy killing. I kept my hand down. I could feel Mr. Brody's gaze on me, but I was forcefully avoiding eye contact. "Kirk?"

I shrugged.

"Well, let's put it this way. For the few of you who bothered to read the book, you'll remember at the end, one character kills another to save him from a painful, degrading death. Euthanasia is putting someone out of his misery. I wished I could have committed euthanasia on these papers."

He dropped my test on my desk. I didn't bother looking at the grade.

On the way out, he called me aside.

"You failed that test."

"Oh."

"You know that book. What's going on with you?"

I shrugged.

"Kirk?"

"I don't know. I had other things on my mind."

"Anything you want to tell me?"

"Not really. I'm just not too interested in schoolwork right now."

"You're not. What are you interested in?"

"Well, mainly having fun." I said it just the way Lauren might say it.

He looked at me kind of sideways, like he was trying to

figure out the real meaning of what I'd just said.

"Thanks for the concern, Mr. Brody. But can I go now?"

"You can do whatever you want, Kirk."

"I can't believe you told Chapelle to go fuck himself," Glenn said. Donna was still laughing. We were in Glenn's car, just driving around at night, celebrating the start of break. Lauren was in the back seat with me. They were all drinking beer.

"Why'd you do that?" Donna asked.

"Well, it seemed like a good idea at the time," I said. Lauren shook her head and smiled at me. "I don't know. I was edgy about some stuff."

"Like what?" Glenn asked.

"Um . . . " I said. Donna turned a little in her seat to see me.

I looked out the window. The windows were all a little fogged, probably from us laughing. The radio was on. I was with friends.

"Well, I'll tell you," I said. And I did. I told them everything about Mom and Hal and California, the pipe, and how the whole thing was starting to get to me. "But you guys have to promise. You can't tell anyone. Not a soul. If anyone finds out at school, it could be over for me. I'm serious. I told you because I trust you."

"Hey, man," Glenn said. "We got your back. Whatever you need."

And I thought about how I had most of what I needed, right there in that car. Or at least that's how it felt.

I was the first to get dropped off. Lauren got out of the car and walked with me to the house. I hadn't left any lights on. The windows were all dark.

"I'll see you tomorrow?" she asked.

"Of course."

"I'm glad you told us."

"Me, too."

After Glenn dropped me off at eleven-thirty, I sat in the dark in my room. I felt I might be able to think more clearly in the dark, I couldn't say why. I had to take stock of the situation. After school, I had paid out one hundred bucks to the plumber after he basically tightened a bolt around a pipe. That was like over a week's pay for me and it was gone in less than an hour. I had about a hundred dollars left in the bank. I didn't want to ask Mom for any money, because she would know I was in a weakened position. Callie was going to pay me, but still. Money was going to be a big, big problem.

And now this thing in school was another real problem. Mr. Horwich said that since we didn't reach my mother, I had to bring her in with me when school started. It was pretty obvious that I had played my last card in trying to fake out Mr. Horwich. I couldn't try to pull another fast one on him. I didn't know how to work that one out, but I'd worry about it later.

At twelve-thirty, the phone rang. At first, I got nervous it might be Mom, because I really didn't want to talk to her, but because I had broken the answering machine, I had set up a code with Lauren and Glenn that they should ring once, hang up, then call right back. There was a pause and then the phone started ringing again, so I knew it was safe to answer. It was Lauren.

"How come you didn't call me?"

"Isn't it too late to call?"

"Not for me. How's it going?"

"Fine. Totally fine."

"Well, okay. I just wanted to check on you."

"Thanks. So I'll see you tomorrow?"

"Yeah. Well. Um." There was a long pause. "Love ya. Bye."

She hung up before I could answer.

Love ya. That's what she said. It wasn't quite I love you, but it was about as close as you can get. It was the low risk version, and then the quick hang up, I guessed, was to make sure she didn't have to chance my not saying it back.

She didn't have to worry.

I would have said it.

I took a shower. The burn on my hand stung. I heard the phone ring, stop, then start ringing. I figured it had to be Lauren again. I got out of the shower fast, grabbed a towel so I wouldn't freeze. It was Glenn.

"What're you doing?" he asked.

"Nothing."

"Good. Then this might be a perfect time for me to beat the crap out of you."

"What'd I do?"

"Do the words 'Dirty Tube Socks' mean anything to you?"

"Yeah. They're what's covering my bedroom floor. Why?"

"Well that's also the name of the band you hooked me up to."

"Oh."

"I didn't ask you to do that."

"Well I thought it was a good thing for you to try."

"Thanks for checking with me first."

"If I checked with you, you wouldn't have done it. Right?"

"Right. Well there was a message waiting for me. I called the guy back. And now I'm set up to audition with them."

"When?"

"Tomorrow."

"That's great. What's your problem, Glenn? Go do it."

"Yeah? And what if they don't want me?"

"They will. But if they don't, then it just wasn't meant to happen. So big deal. You ever hear the expression 'Nothing ventured, nothing gained'?"

"You ever hear the expression 'You're a big pain in the ass'? It's no skin off your butt. How would you like it if someone told you *you* sucked?"

"Gee, Glenn. I can't relate to that feeling at all."

"I don't know why you did this. I won't know what to play."

"How about one of the million songs you can play note-perfect? Gimme a break. You're gonna knock their dirty tube socks off."

"I'd better."

"I'll go with you, if you want."

"Okay. If you want, you can come."

"Sounds good."

I hung up the phone. I dried off and got into sweats. I went down and had a chocolate doughnut. I spread out on the living room floor. Moonlight came in through the window. I thought a little bit about what Callie had told me about, with the moonlight on the running water. The water changes. The moonlight stays.

Let the water run. I'd still be there.

Since Lauren was going with her family to her grandmother's for the holiday, we decided to get together the day before she was leaving on Christmas Eve. She didn't live far, so I walked over. I stopped in town first and bought her a little necklace with her name on it. Her stepfather answered the door. He was what people call a beefy man. He had a big fleshy nose that was pink with a road map of broken blood vessels. He had tiny eyes and short white-blond hair.

"Nice to meet you, Mr. Mason."

"Good to meet you, Kurt," he said, shaking my hand. "So what are you planning to do with my daughter?"

Somehow I got the idea that this required a serious answer. Joking around, saying something like, "Well, I'm planning to defile her in ways that would embarrass porno stars," I'd probably quickly end up as a big blood spot on the front step.

"Oh, maybe pizza? A matinee?"

"Sounds fine to me. Honey? Kurt's here." He turned to me and grinned. I now knew what snaggleteeth were. "So, Kurt. You have big plans for the holidays?"

"Nothing very unusual. Kind of low-key. Stay home, quality time."

"Sounds perfect. And here she is."

She really looked great to me. I felt an excited feeling, like a rush of adrenaline when I saw her. There I was picking her up. My girlfriend. Was this me, or did I somehow step into somebody else's life?

Once we got back to my house, I gave her the necklace, which she seemed to like. I put it on for her. I have to say, when she turned her back to me and lifted her hair for me to fasten the clasp, the sight of the back of her neck was kind of sexy. I never would have thought of the back of a girl's neck as a sexy spot, but there you go. I was learning quite a lot, really.

We listened to the radio for a while, holding hands. She turned to me and looked at me.

"What?" I asked.

"You're just not at all like any of the other guys I know."

"Believe me, you're not like any girls I know."

So then, of course, we started fooling around. And it got pretty hot again. The couch was too uncomfortable.

We went up to my room. We got pretty worked up again and she pulled her jeans totally off and dropped them on the floor next to my bed. All she had on was her underwear.

I couldn't believe this was happening. This must have been what she meant about just wanting to get fun out of life. It suddenly seemed like a really great philosophy.

She was moving against my hand, hard, hard, and kind of panting and making a sound deep in her throat. It sounded a little like a frustrated sound.

"I want you to . . . " she kind of whispered, panted.

"What?" I said. It was kind of hard to find my voice.

She gripped my hand and furrowed her eyebrows. She squeezed my wrist and pulled away. "Okay. Come on."

And she took her underwear off. And she held her arms out to me.

lonely

I had gone to the drugstore earlier in the week, just to make sure I was ready in case it happened. Now that the time had come, I got the condom on without too much of a problem. To be honest, I had practiced with six of them in the afternoon, just to make sure I knew what I was doing. So that went okay.

She took me and guided me. I couldn't quite believe it was happening. But it was.

Lauren was really having a pretty intense time. She was wrapped around me, squeezing with every bit of her. Her legs, her arms, everything. Maybe it was because I was really naïve, or just so inexperienced, but I really didn't know that girls could like sex as much as she did. I mean, everyone knows that guys are basically horndogs, but I just didn't expect her to want it so much, and to get so into it.

But the way she was breathing, the sounds she was making, really kind of threw me. It was almost hard to tell if she was having a good time or was in some kind of pain or something. Yeah, I've seen the movies and all that, but this wasn't like anything I'd seen. And it was a little hard to know what was going on with her. At one point I slowed down, and when I looked at her, I was pretty sure she was crying.

"Are you okay?" I asked.

She nodded.

"What's wrong?"

"Nothing. Come on. Go."

She started moving against me, slowly, but hard with strong movements. I fell into her rhythm. And when she was moving faster, harder, she pulled my head next to hers, her fist twisted in my hair.

My mind couldn't fix on any thoughts, they just went racing by. Words flashed through my inner voice, spinning like the inside of a hurricane. This is it, you're having sex, was one thought that kept coming back to me. *Love* came and went.

Then my mind went totally blank as I finished.

Her legs pulled so hard against the backs of my thighs I thought she might actually dislocate both of my hips.

She held me tight and she wouldn't let go. It was like her life depended on it. She was panting, and kind of crying and laughing all at once.

It was this totally pure emotion and it was so intense that even I got a little scared by it.

And so we lay in bed for about an hour after she finally let me go, and we watched this horrible sitcom from, like, thirty-five years ago. There was something so not-funny and kind of sad about those early seventies sitcoms. They just really depressed me.

Lauren noticed that my fingers looked horrible. I had been biting the skin around the nails, which is something I do when I'm kind of edgy. Instead of letting them heal, I work at the little edges of skin and make it all worse. Lauren looked at my fingers, which were all raw, ragged, and basically pretty gross, I had to admit. Still, she held my hands while we watched TV.

I took Lauren home, wished her a merry Christmas. She told me to wait a minute. She went in and came out with a small wrapped package. I opened it. It was a pair of black leather gloves. They were a lot nicer than my wool gloves. I thanked her and moved toward her. She looked inside, pulled the door closed, and then gave me a soft, slow kiss.

I pulled on the gloves and walked home, hunched forward into the wind.

My mind was kind of spinning when I got home. I had actually had sex, which I guess is like a real milestone, usually. But the whole thing was so different from what I expected. I mean, sure, physically it was great and all that, but I didn't know what to make of Lauren's behavior. It would seem like a turn-on that she would get so into it, but what about the crying? And what about the way she held on to me? I didn't have any experience to compare it to of course, but it seemed to be something way beyond physical passion. And I couldn't really ask her about it. I could have called Glenn, but he knew her, and that didn't seem right. I wasn't about to discuss it with Callie.

I was confused and full of questions. I didn't have anyone to talk to.

The phone rang. It wasn't the code, and somehow I believed it was Mom. I couldn't deal with the idea of talking to her. I stared at the phone as it rang and rang. Finally it stopped and the house was silent. Silent, except for the echo of the ring that stuck in my mind.

I changed my sheets and got into bed.

I couldn't sleep.

I was totally wired.

I got out my little notebook and began to write.

Alone. A lone kid. A lonely time.
Time alone
Time together, our together time
Somehow makes me feel alone
Are you alone, where you are?
I'm alone here.
We're together in being alone.

 Why do you scream, why do you shout?
 I cannot understand what that's about.
 You seemed in pain, I cannot name
 Whether it's from in or out
Now you have shown
The passion you own
Please explain my role.

You held my hand,
Please understand
I'm so thrilled I could scream and shout
But this love thing, Again, I ask, for the millionth time,
Where do I fit in?

I read over my writing and it embarrassed me. It wasn't good, and it didn't explain how I felt. The writing failed me. It didn't help to define anything.

I slept until the phone woke me up.

"You have to drive," Glenn said.

"What?"

"The audition. You have to drive."

"Calm down. What time is it?"

"It's twelve-thirty. You're taking me."

"I can't drive. You know I just have my permit."

"You're gonna have to. My sister took my car to work and left me stranded. Just get in your car and drive over here. Go a regular speed, don't do anything stupid, and you'll be fine. You got me into this, now you gotta help me out."

"All right, okay. I'll be there in ten minutes."

"And bring explosives. On the way back we're gonna pay my sister a little visit at work and blow up the whole damn roller rink."

I was pretty nervous at first, getting behind the wheel. But then I figured, there was no reason for me to get stopped. Cops didn't have X-ray vision to see through my car door into my wallet where I had a learner's permit instead of a license. As long as I stayed relaxed and drove normally, I'd be fine.

I got to Glenn's without any problems. He was standing outside, guitar case slung over his shoulder. He had on his leather jacket, a black watch cap, and his hair tied back in a ponytail. He looked pretty cool.

He kept cracking his knuckles all the way to the house, which was one town over. As we got out of the car, we heard drums pounding and the heavy throb of a bass, the rip of guitar chords hit hard.

The three guys in the basement looked like clones of Glenn's friends. One guy who seemed to be the leader had so much hair that I was trying to figure out if it might actually be a wig. He tilted his head forward enough for his hair to fall over his face, then he whipped it back over his head. I got the feeling he had spent a lot of time practicing this in the mirror. He said hi, told Glenn to set up and show them what he could do.

Glenn was all business. He plugged in, checked his tuning, and went right into a set of classic rock stuff and some other stuff I didn't really know. As far as I could tell, he was amazingly good. Glenn finished up with "All along the Watchtower" and a feedback-filled final chord.

The kids huddled together and whispered.

He looked at me. I nodded to him.

"Hey, man. You sing?" one of the kids asked.

"A little. I can carry a tune."

"Cool. Well, you're a Sock, if you wanna be."

Glenn smiled.

―――――

"Are you cool with the plan?" Glenn asked as I drove him home.

"What plan is that?"

"Well, are you disappointed that this band plays mainly covers?"

"Why would I be?"

"Well, what about all the stuff we worked on?"

"I don't know. I never imagined that stuff being played by a band, with people I don't know. I like it the way you do it. Your music. My words. Your voice."

"I don't have too great a voice."

"I think it's just right for our stuff." From my peripheral vision, I could see him look over at me. He opened his mouth to say something, but couldn't seem to get the words out. He turned and looked out the window.

"That's good to hear."

I started to speak, but my voice caught, too. I was kind of surprised at a feeling of emotion like that.

We rode in silence to his house. When I dropped Glenn off, he was grumbling that he was expected to hang around with his "totally lame" family. "Hey. At least you have a family," I said.

"True. As bad as things are for me, they could be worse. I could be you," he said.

So much for sentimentality.

When I got home, I got out some spray cleaner and a few rags and started cleaning up around the house a little bit. It was starting to get kind of grimy, and though I've never exactly been the neatest kid around, I could kind of see how things could just go to hell if you didn't keep after it.

The phone rang, stopped, then rang. It was Lauren.

"I was just thinking about you," I said.

"Really? I've been thinking about you a lot. I really miss you."

"You, too. I mean, I miss you, too."

"I'm going crazy here. It's so boring. I wish you were here."

"What would we do?" I asked.

She laughed. "Can't say."

"That's not what I meant."

"Mmm. It's what I'd want to do."

"There's someone in the room?"

"That's correct," she said. "But you know what I'm thinking, don't you?"

"I'm pretty sure I do."

"Well, that's on the schedule for very soon."

"I can't wait."

"Me either."

We talked a little bit about the things she was doing (going to mall after mall, even though they were absolutely packed the day before Christmas, and sitting around her grandmother's house while the guys watched TV) and how bored she was with all of it.

"I just would so rather be there with you," she said.

"Do they know about me?"

"I'd say, yeah. I talk about you practically all the time. They're calling me Loopy. Or Lauren in Love."

Did she just say "in love"? Did I hear that right?

"What was that?" I asked.

"In love? Yeah?"

"Nothing," I said. Was I missing something? Did things just move to another level and nobody told me?

"I get this way." She covered the mouthpiece, then came back on. "I'm gonna have to get off. My idiot brother wants to use the phone."

"All right. Well I'll see you the day after tomorrow, right?"

"I don't know if I can make it that long. I'm missing you like crazy. I'm thinking about you every minute."

"Me, too," I said.

She said "Love ya," again before hanging up, but this time, she didn't hang up. She waited for me to say "You, too."

Which, at the time, I guessed was probably true.

As I got back to my cleaning, I started to wonder what she meant by "I get this way," which seemed to mean that she had been in love before. I guess that wasn't so surprising, and I tried not to think about it, but it seemed pretty clear that she must have had sex before. But I was a little surprised to hear that she had been in love before. Maybe I was being unreasonable, but somehow I had kind of imagined that she hadn't really found anyone that she could be in love with before.

A while back, Callie had asked me to look for a book called *Eleven Kinds of Loneliness*. She read it when she was seventeen and really liked it. She warned me that it would be hard to find, but I got it through interlibrary loan.

Loneliness on loan, I thought. We read four of the stories and I have to say, the title was pretty accurate.

The stories were depressing, but they sure did get the feelings of loneliness right. One story was called "A Glutton for Punishment" and it was about this guy who, when he was a kid playing with the other kids, always liked to be the one who got killed. He made up these dramatic death scenes. Later, when he's an adult, he gets this thrill from all his failures. It gets so he enjoys failing more than succeeding. After I finished reading it, both Callie and I were totally silent.

Callie didn't have any cooking to do for the stores, so she had cooked just for us. It was a gumbo, and it was just the right thing for a cold night.

"So what do you have planned for tomorrow?" she asked.

"Nothing much."

"Just you and mom?"

"Mm." To tell the truth, I was starting to feel kind of crappy about not telling her what my situation was. It was a secret I felt I still had to keep from her, but I didn't like it. "How about you?"

"Well, some friends may drop by. Like I said, I don't make too big a thing of Christmas."

"Me either."

"But . . . " she said, getting up. She went into the other room for a minute and came back with a pretty big box.

"Oh, wow," I said. I had been trying to think about something to get for her and I had come up blank. Then the whole thing happened at school and I didn't get to get her anything. "That's nice, but I don't have your present with me. It's not . . . done yet."

"That's okay. Just open it. I can't wait to see what you think."

It was the best collection of books. There was stuff on Zen and Eastern thought, collected stories of Hemingway, collected stories of Fitzgerald, a really beautiful leather-covered collection of all of Shakespeare's plays, a book called *Free Your Poet*, and a book called *The Courage to Write*.

"I know it's a cliché, but you really shouldn't have."

"Are you kidding? It was my pleasure." She stood up and put her arms out. I stood and we hugged.

"Thanks so much," I said.

"No. Thank you."

When I got home, there was an Express Mail envelope leaning against the front door. I went in and opened it. It was an airplane ticket to Los Angeles. There was a note inside:

> I've been trying to call, but there's no answer. Something may be wrong with the machine.
> This is an open-end ticket. I know what you said about coming. I can't help but think that this is some kind of point you're trying to make. If you're trying to make me

feel guilty, to make me feel like a bad mother, you're too late. I don't need your help in that department. I can do it all on my own. But I do know one thing: I can't be a good mother when I'm miserable, and that's what I was and will be in New Jersey. Give me a chance out here. I think everything will be different. In a good way.

You're smart. I have faith in you and I have faith that you're smart enough to do the right thing, which is to come here. Call me at this number when you know which flight you're taking. I'll meet you at the airport.

Love, me

I put the ticket back in the envelope and left it on the little table by the door. Not interested.

I sat in my living room and looked at all the books Callie gave me. I wanted to get her something really nice, but I just couldn't think of anything that would be right. Obviously, books weren't a good idea. Jewelry seemed wrong. Clothes, wrong. Maybe some kind of cooking instrument, but I wouldn't have a clue what kind, or where to get it. Every book she picked for me was perfect. Whatever I got her would have to be something that showed thought. And then the thought came to me.

I drove to the only supermarket I could find that was open late on Christmas Eve. It was twenty-five minutes away, but I was getting pretty comfortable driving. I pushed my cart down the aisles and made my selections, not skimping. No generics. Only the best stuff. As far as I could tell.

I got some great cooking ideas by reading the labels on the bottles in the spice section. Some said things like "For use with beef, lamb, pork," some said "Use in stews and casseroles," some said "For marinades and roasts." Since I was going to make kind of a combo deal, I picked up exactly the right spices.

I spent the whole morning and into the early afternoon cooking.

At around noon, Lauren called.

"I can't wait to get home and see you," she said.

"Me too." I was trying to clean shrimp, but I wasn't sure exactly what I was supposed to be getting rid of besides the shell.

"What are you doing?"

"I'm cooking, believe it or not."

"Cooking what?"

"I'm cooking something for Callie."

"The woman you read to. Do you call her Callie or Miss Whatever?"

"I call her Callie."

"Hm," she said. There was something a little weird in her voice. "So you're cooking for Callie. That's sweet. When are you going to cook for me?"

"For you? Whenever you want. I'll let you know how this comes out."

"What's the matter with you?" she asked.

"What do you mean?"

"You sound kind of funny."

"Well, to tell you the truth, I'm kind of right in the middle of this cooking project. I'm sort of concentrating."

"Okay. Well, anyway. I'll see you tomorrow, then."

"Yeah. Tomorrow."

"Great. Have a good time with Callie." She really had a little bit of a tone there, which was totally uncalled for. All in all, I was really a little surprised at Lauren. Whatever, I had my hands full.

I'll admit, the kitchen was becoming a mess. I had just about every pot out, but I knew the key was to cook each part separately, so each thing kept its original flavor. I made sure to keep the chutney chicken, the burgundy-soaked beef, the shrimp, the potatoes, the pearl onions, the clove-studded sausage all separate. They had to stay separate, right until the big mix.

"Callie? It's Kirk."

"Oh, hi."

"Listen, are those friends of yours over there?"

"No."

"Oh, great. Because I thought I might stop by for a little, if that's okay."

"Oh, no. Really, I'm sure you want to spend the day with your mother."

"What's wrong?"

"Nothing."

"You sound kind of down or something. Everything okay?"

"Yup."

"So can I come over?"

"I'm just kind of lying around."

"Well, perfect. Can I come?"

"Fine."

There was no way I could carry the two full pots all the way to Callie's, so I put them on the floor in the back seat of the car. I drove very slowly to make sure nothing spilled. I had to be really careful, but I was able to carry one pot in each arm and ring her bell. After a moment, Callie opened the door.

"Hi!" I said.

"Oh my God. Did someone dump garbage on my front walk?"

"Huh?" I turned around. "No. I don't see anything."

"Jeez. All right, hurry up, come in. Let's get this door closed."

Callie closed the door behind me. I stood to the side and put the pots down on the table next to the door, being as silent as I could. I wanted to surprise her.

"Whew. Kirk, did you step in something on your way over?"

I checked the bottom of my boots.

"No," I said.

"Really? Is the door completely closed? I can still smell that. What a stench!"

"I don't smell anything," I said. Then I looked at the pots with my cooking.

Oh.

"I think I'm going to vomit," she said. "Jesus, what in the hell is that? I'm gagging."

"You know, I think there was a dead thing on your lawn. Like a woodchuck or something."

"Oh. That could be it."

"Let me go check it out. I'll be right back."

I pushed the door open and silently took my pots. I pitched my cooking into the bushes.

I pulled my boots off after I closed the door.

"I got rid of it. I used a stick."

"Thanks."

She was lying on the couch. That's when I saw that she didn't look good.

"Callie? What's wrong?"

"Nothing."

"Really? You don't look too good at all. Are you sick or something?"

"No, I'm fine. I'm just a little down."

"Didn't your friends come to see you?"

"I wasn't having anyone over. I sometimes just don't feel like seeing people around holidays. It's really nothing. It happens every year."

"I kind of feel the same way, sometimes."

She gave me a kind of weak smile. She sighed. "Also, Ted called."

"Ted the fiancé guy, you mean?"

"Yes, Ted the fiancé guy."

"Oh. I guess it wasn't too great a conversation."

"Not too."

"Oh."

There was a long silence.

"I don't know," she finally said.

"Don't know what?"

"Nothing. I'm just . . . why am I alone?"

"You aren't. I'm here."

She looked at me. I mean, she didn't look at me. But it was *like* she looked at me. She smiled a little. "I know. And that's good. But it's not what I meant."

"I know."

There was another long silence. She looked so miserable.

"You know, thanks for coming to cheer me up, but I think I'd rather just be alone. I'm not a lot of fun to be around when I'm like this."

I watched her. She looked so small, lying on the couch that way. The look on her face really killed me.

"Hey. Is there a phone upstairs?"

"Sure."

"Could I use it for an emergency private phone call?"

Callie's bedroom was very plain. It had a big bed with a plain bedspread. Two dressers, and a small night table. I picked up the phone and dialed.

"What are you doing right now?" I asked.

"Nothing. We ate and now I'm sitting around and pretending I don't hate my whole family," Glenn said.

"Great. I need a favor," I said.

"Get your shoes on," I told Callie.

"What?"

"Hurry up. We're going out."

"What are you talking about? I'm not going anywhere."

"Yes. You are. Let's move."

"Where do you think we're going on Christmas?"

"You'll see," I said. "You'll see."

Glenn and Donna were already there, waiting at the back door. I introduced them to Callie.

"Nice to meet you," Callie said. "Maybe you'll tell me where we are."

"Sorry, not allowed to yet," Donna said.

"Glenn?" Callie asked.

"Can't. Midget's orders. Come here, Napoleon." Glenn pulled me aside, his hand on my shoulder. "I have to pay her now. She's not happy about this."

I handed Glenn the hundred dollars I had taken out from the ATM on the way over. That was pretty much the rest of my money. I was down to my last hundred or so. But this was important. I would have spent my last dime to do this. "Nothing bad's gonna happen. It's cool," I said.

"I don't know if it's cool, but it sure is you," he said. "Go in. I'll deal with this and then I'll be there."

"Thanks, pal." I looked at him. He shrugged.

"What is this place?" Callie asked when I guided her inside. "It has a pretty big echo."

"That's right. So, Callie. Can you roller skate?"

Donna had to skate with Callie in the beginning. Glenn

and I were falling all over the place. Like I said, I'm not the most coordinated. We only had one tiny light on in the whole place, so nobody from the street would see that anybody was inside, and Glenn's sister wouldn't get fired for letting us in.

After a while, I could stay up without falling, sort of. I was wobbly, but at least I was vertical. I took Callie's hand. Donna went to help Glenn.

Callie was actually a pretty good skater. In the low light of the roller rink, she couldn't see anything at all, not even shapes. She was completely in the dark, but still, she kept me upright. I told her when we were coming to the turns.

We went around and around, relaxing into it. Getting a rhythm and flowing with it.

It was so great to hear her laugh, which echoed off the walls, and filled the huge space.

truth

The next day I told Callie everything. We were at her kitchen table. We had just finished two bowls of chicken stew with dumplings, and I was warm and full and I had to tell her. So I explained about Hal, and about Mom, and California. She listened without saying anything, except when she needed me to clarify something. Sometimes she seemed to stare at a point on the tabletop, at other times it looked like she was holding eye contact with me.

"So that's what's been going on," I said. "It's pretty bad."

She nodded and poured herself a glass of water. She took two long sips and put it down gently on the table.

"So what are you going to do?" she asked.

"I don't know. But I'm not just going along with it. I'm going to fight it."

"How?"

"I don't know. But I'm not going to let it all happen. I'm just not."

She nodded a couple of times and lifted her glass. "Kirk, here's a question for you. Can you control water?"

"What do you mean?"

"Just what I said. Can you control water?"

She held the glass of water about a foot above the surface of the table and began to tilt the glass. I was confused—she was about to spill it all out. She kept tilting and I put my hand against the mouth of the glass, my other hand against the bottom of the glass. The water welled up against my hand, and I held it back.

She straightened out the glass and I took my hands away. "Okay," she said. "You controlled that, right? So you can control a little water. You're stronger than water."

"I guess so."

She took my hand and held it above the table, palm up. "Control this. Hold the water."

She poured the water into my hand, and kept pouring. It spilled out of my hand and all over the tabletop. "Control it, Kirk. Hold tight. Squeeze. You're stronger."

"You're making a big mess," I said.

"That's okay. It doesn't bother me." She finished pouring until the glass was empty. "It's just water. The water doesn't fight. It flows. Water is soft, but it can wear away stone. Could you fight a flood? Could you control a rainstorm?"

"I guess not. I get it, go with the flow and all that. But what do you want me to do? Just give up everything that's important to me?"

"I'm not saying just give up," she said. "You heard the old saying about how the big rigid tree will be destroyed in

208

a rainstorm, while the little flexible tree will move with the wind and survive." She traced a finger through the beaded puddles on the table, drawing long trails of water, blending them. "I'm saying that if you just dig in and fight, you're going to lose this. You can't control it."

"Why not?"

"Because control is an illusion. Things happen, Kirk. Believe me, I know. You can't *control* life."

I got to Glenn's around eight. Lauren was in a great mood, and she was smiling and laughing a lot more than usual. It made her really attractive. It made her eyes look so bright and lively.

It turned out that they had been getting high for about an hour before I got there, and by the time I arrived, they were done and wanted to eat. So Glenn drove us to the diner.

I was not having a good time at the diner. The three of them were laughing on and on about something that totally escaped me. They had been doing it since we got there, and to tell the truth, it made me not feel too much like being with them. I smiled, but I wasn't in on any of the jokes. I was the fourth person, but I felt like a fifth wheel.

I was thinking about what Callie had said. It was pretty interesting, the idea of how rigid can be weak, but fluid and yielding can be strong. It was a cool idea.

Glenn and I took the check to the cashier. When I opened up my wallet, I realized I was in trouble. I couldn't figure out where all the money had gone. I actually had to count out change to make the check, and I ended up with eight cents left over.

As Glenn drove, I was caught up in trying to remember whether I had twenty-four dollars and change or fourteen dollars and change left in the bank account. I just couldn't remember. Definitely not too much. I wasn't about to ask Mom for money. I wasn't going to ask her for anything. I shook my head and looked at Lauren. She was gazing at me.

"What?" I said.

"Nothing. I just like watching you when you're deep in thought. What, are you composing a poem or something like that?"

If you only knew.

Glenn dropped us at my house. As we went up the walkway, Lauren said, "It's so cool that your mother's not here. You can do whatever you want." I thought it was pretty odd that she thought I had all this freedom, and to me, it felt like for the big things in my life, I pretty much had no decent choices at all. I was kind of surprised that Lauren didn't get it.

But still, once I closed the door, it took about eight seconds before we were locked together like we were epoxied at the mouth. We fought to get our clothes off. I heard material rip more than once. We just both seemed frantic, like we were running out of time.

It was pretty great.

Then, after, there was this long holding time when she wouldn't let go at all. It felt good and all that, though I was sleepy and I actually could have taken a nap. But I had the feeling that going to sleep after doing it was bad form or something. So I forced myself to stay awake.

She was looking at me again.

"What are you thinking?" she asked.

I was actually thinking about something she'd said days before: "I get like this." Meaning, emotional about guys. And, I figured, it also meant heavy into sex, with other guys. Somehow, I had believed that the way she felt about me was something different, something specific to us. But what she'd said made me think that there had been guys she was intense about before me, and there would be guys she'd be intense about after me. Maybe I was one in a series, maybe the whole thing was just another way for her to have fun. There might not have been as much to us as I'd thought.

The other thing was that when we were all together at the diner, I felt so different from them. I felt like an out-sider. And though I guessed I felt close to Lauren when we were locked up in bed, now that it was over, I just felt totally disconnected from her.

"Come on. What are you thinking about?"

"I don't know. It's just that you and Donna and Glenn have been friends for a while. And sometimes I feel a little like an outsider when we're together."

"You're completely in the group now." She laughed and shook her head. "I don't even know what you're talking about."

That was exactly my point. I didn't think it would be worth talking about anymore.

"What are you thinking now?" she asked.

"I'm thinking about how great it is to be with you," I said.

Right answer. I could tell by the way she wrapped around me. It was the right answer, but not the true one.

I had to ask Callie for help. I told her I needed to talk to her about something and it was pretty important. She said I could come over right away.

"I just need a little advance to tide me over for a while."

"Don't worry about it," she said. She walked to her desk and took out a checkbook and this metal stencil kind of thing. She put a check in it and folded a metal plate over the check. It had slots in it so she could write in the correct places on the check.

"Four hundred? Five? What would help?"

"Oh, not that much. Just like about eighty will do it."

She smiled. "I'll make it five hundred. Don't worry about it. Have you talked to your Mom recently?"

"I'm not answering the phone."

"You can't hide from her, Kirk."

"I can try," I said, trying to laugh a little and make it sound like a joke.

"She is still your mother. You're going to have to work your problems out sooner or later." She finished signing the check and handed it to me.

"Thanks, really. Um. This has to clear or something?"

"It should clear in about three days," she said.

"Oh. Okay." Three days. Could I make it three days?

"But hang on. I have some cash."

I couldn't say anything. I wanted to say no thanks, but I actually really needed the money. I didn't even have any food in the house.

I felt sick to my stomach as she handed me sixty dollars, three twenties folded the long way.

She smiled as she handed the money to me.

I wasn't smiling. I was sick about it.

I felt like a little boy taking his allowance.

I was glad she couldn't see me.

I knew Callie was right when she said it was wrong to not answer the phone. I could handle it. I was going to try Callie's approach and try to be a little more flexible, stop fighting so hard. So I did pick up the phone when it rang, trying not to feel anxious.

"So guess what?" Mom said. It was funny how clear the connection was. It sounded like she was calling from down the street. You'd never know she was a whole continent away from me.

"I don't know."

"You'll never guess."

"You joined a cult."

"Very funny."

"Isn't that what they do out there? Join cults and surf and get plastic surgery?"

"Yes. You're right. That's all everybody does out here. You know it all."

"Okay. I give up."

"This is really good. Really good. I'm in a program."

"What, you went to a taping?"

"No. A program. I'm not drinking."

That was not what I expected her to say. In fact, in a million years, I never expected to hear those words from her mouth.

"Well that's really fantastic. Congratulations."

"Sixteen days. I didn't say anything before because I wanted to get past the two week point. I can do this."

"That's really something. I'm proud of you." I was.

"I told you I was getting things under control."

"Well I'm glad."

"And the restaurant deal may actually go through. Hal had such a great idea. How would you like to be a valet?"

"What, you mean like a butler?"

"No. I mean a parking valet at the restaurant. You could make a lot of money. This could be so nice. A real family business. Oh, and also. Hal and I think we might have found a nice place to live. It's not too far from the beach. You can kind of see the ocean if you lean out the window."

"Sounds great."

There was a silence.

"So . . . " she said.

"Yes I got the ticket, no I'm not coming."

There was a long pause and she exhaled a long breath. I wondered if she was smoking.

"Well, you're going to have to come. I spoke to Maggie McDonnell. I listed the house with her."

"Listed it in what? The list of houses in the worst need of a paint job in the county?"

"No, I listed it. I put it on the market. To be sold."

"You *what*?"

"I'm selling the house."

"You can't!"

"Of course I can. And I am. So unless you plan to start living at the Y, you're going to have to bite the bullet, use the ticket, and trust that I can make things good for us out here."

"But I still live here."

"Not for long, baby. I'm sorry, but I think it's time I finally got tough about this. It's for your own good. Like I said, you're going to have to trust me."

I couldn't do it anymore. "I'll tell you the truth. After all this, I don't know if I'll ever trust you again."

I wanted her back, but not anymore
Can't stand her voice as
I lose all my choices
How do I flow? How do I bend?
How long can I sway if the storm never ends?

I wasn't having a good time making out with my girlfriend. Here was a really attractive girl who really liked me and was willing to do stuff with me, *wanted* to do stuff with me, and God knows I was in no position to be choosy, but I was kind of just not into it. I wasn't at all excited, to be kind of blunt.

There we were, on my bed, kissing and everything and I wondered what I was doing it for. The thing was, she liked me, definitely. And it may sound egotistical to say, but she liked me a lot more than I guess I liked her. So we did stuff, but I was starting to feel pretty much like I was really taking advantage of the situation and damn me if it didn't ruin the whole thing.

"What's wrong?" she asked. She pulled back a couple of inches. Her eyes were dark, dark brown. They were wide and you could look deep into them. Except, I felt like I couldn't look into her eyes at all, right then.

"I'm sorry. I should have told you. I think I'm getting a cold or something. We probably shouldn't be doing this. I don't want to get you sick."

"Oh."

The phone rang. It was Glenn.

"Dude! We got a gig. We're playing a bar in, like, a week. Live, baby."

"Excellent."

"I'm coming over, tell you all about it."

"It's Glenn," I told Lauren.

"Who's that? The hobbit princess?"

"Yep."

"Oh, sorry. Forget it. Wouldn't want to interrupt hobbit nookie."

"No, you can come. It's fine."

"Even better. I'll bring Donna."

"Fine."

Lauren didn't seem to mind that I invited Glenn over.

Glenn and Donna got to my place about twenty minutes later. They had a case of beer with them.

They made themselves comfortable, popped open their beers. Lauren took one. Glenn went on about the band

("Way cool"), how they played together ("Tight"), and the gig ("This totally happening club two towns over").

"Sounds great," I said. "A perfect match."

"There's just one thing, though," he said. "The lead singer, Sean? He's kind of a dick. He thinks he's Steven Tyler or something. He's all into this drama. His voice is okay, but he lays it all on too thick. It's kind of embarrassing. He wears, like, tights and scarves. He looks more like Stevie Nicks than Steve Tyler."

"Well, at least you're in a band, right?"

"I guess," he said. "I played them a couple of the things we wrote. They were into it. They wanted to learn them, but I said I needed to do them solo. So they said it would be okay with them, but they wanted to give some kind of back-up. I said I needed to think about it. Either way, like we said, I'll still sing. What do you think?"

"No problem for me," I said.

"Cool." He opened another beer, and said, "By the way, feel free."

What the hell, I thought. One beer won't kill me. I took one myself, and gave one to Lauren. I didn't much love it, but I got used to it. Glenn couldn't stop talking about the Tube Socks and how this was the best thing that had happened to him in a long time.

I was midway through my second beer when there was a knock on the door. I got up and opened it. Four of Glenn's friends were standing there.

"Hey," one of them said.

"Hey," I said.

"Is, uh, Glenn here?"

"Right here," Glenn said. "What are you doing here?"

"You said you were comin' over here."

"Yeah, but I didn't tell you that you could come."

"Come on, it took us half an hour to get here. My ride's heater's busted, dude. We froze to get here."

"That's your problem. This isn't my place."

"It's okay. Come on in," I said.

"Cool. Lemme just get the brews out of my trunk."

We stopped letting people in when the fifth group showed up. Apparently there was some grapevine that was so fast, you'd think the phone company had hotlines set up all over town. It looked like there were more than twenty people milling around the house, beer bottles all over the place, the stereo up pretty loud.

I didn't know too many of the people, but they seemed pretty happy to see me. The beers I had been drinking probably had a little to do with my easygoing attitude.

I couldn't remember the last time I had been to a decent party that didn't involve blowing out birthday candles. I had been to a couple in, like, eighth grade, but they could hardly be called decent, unless decent means standing around and drinking Pepsi out of a crackly plastic cup while most of the other kids disappeared in pairs into the dark of the Ping-Pong room.

I couldn't remember ever seeing so many people in the house. There had to be thirty. The best thing was seeing so many people having a good time in my place. It seemed alive.

The bathroom had a line four people deep. I wasn't used to the urinary consequences of beer. I couldn't wait. I went out the back door and peed in the bushes. And that's when I saw a problem.

I shut the door behind me and ran into the living room. I switched off the stereo. There was a bunch of protests. I stood up on the coffee table, my heart pounding.

"Everyone shut up. There's a police car pulling up in front of the house."

It got quiet very fast.

"Glenn, look between the curtains. Is it still there?"

Glenn peeked between the curtains. "Yup, he's there."

"Oh, man. Okay. All of you guys, get in the kitchen. Hurry up."

Most of the kids started moving right away. They obviously had done this before, because each of them grabbed three or four beer bottles. Glenn and Donna started clearing away the rest.

"Coming up the walk, Kirk. You got ten seconds."

"Shit. Lauren, come here." I told her what to do.

I opened the door the second time they knocked. Be straight, be straight, be straight, I told myself.

"Hi," I said, putting on a confused face.

"Evening. How are you this evening?"

"Fine. Yourself?"

"Fine. We got a noise complaint from down the street."

"Really? About this house? Because you can see, it's pretty quiet here."

"Uh-huh. You wouldn't be having some kind of party, now would you?"

"Well, actually we're having a study group." I held open the door for him, revealing Lauren, Glenn, Donna, and two other kids sitting around the living room, all with books in their hands. The books just happened to be on Zen and Eastern thought, collected stories of Fitzgerald, a really beautiful leather-covered collection of all of Shakespeare's plays and *The Courage to Write*.

I held up *The Collected Stories of Hemingway*, which I had in my hand. "We're looking for the motif of the Fencing Prince in the works of Hemingway and Fitzgerald. We have a test as soon as we get back to school."

"Uh-huh," the cop said. He took another look at the model students studying so hard in the living room. "Are your parents home?"

"Well, I'll tell you the truth, officer. My father left when I was a kid. And my mother, well, it's a little bit of a sensitive issue, you see. The truth of it is that my mother sometimes tends to, you know, drink a tiny bit too much at social occasions, and she was at an Eve of New Year's Eve party tonight and she had just a tad much. That's why I asked my classmates if we could move the study group here. So I could help her if she needed anything."

"That's very responsible of you. Is she all right?"

"Sleeping it off, I hope." I gave him a little smile that said, What can you do?

"Well, all right, then. Maybe all the noise was coming from the other party down the block. You take care of your mom, then."

"Thank you. I will. Good night."

He nodded to me and turned. "Oh, and one other thing," he said, turning back. He leaned over my shoulder. "Good luck on that test, kids."

When I woke up in the morning, there was a pounding in my head that would have made the torture methods used in the Spanish Inquisition seem like child's play. I had finished all my puking by about nine in the morning. That was after making deals with God that I'd never drink again in my whole life if he let me live through this.

I went back to bed and switched between dozing and trying to convince the little man with the sledgehammer to stop slamming away at the inside of my skull. At around one, there was a knock on the door. I figured it must be Lauren, who I took home at around two. I staggered downstairs and opened the door.

Glenn and Donna stood there, looking perfectly fine.

"You're looking good," he said as he moved past me.

"Aspirin will help," Donna said, patting my cheek and following Glenn. They were super-efficient at cleaning up. They even came with a bunch of big plastic garbage bags. I still felt a lot better lying flat, so I eased facedown onto the couch.

"Puke?" Glenn asked.

"I think my pancreas came up."

"Excellent. Make deals with God?"

"You've done that, too?"

"Oh, once or twice. Got a tiny bit of a headache?"

"Oh, just a wee one."

"Yeah. You'll live."

They cleaned up so well that the place looked better than it had before the party.

"Lauren didn't call you yet, did she?" Glenn asked.

"No. Why?"

"She won't for a while. She gets wicked hangovers," Donna said. "Alcohol affects her pretty strong."

"I know the feeling," I said.

She found something under the couch, something curled and leathery-looking. She held it up to show me.

"No idea," I said. She shrugged and threw it in the garbage bag.

I stood up and my head pounded. I sat back down on the couch.

"A quart of water and four hours sleep. You'll be good as new," Donna said. She kissed my forehead and they left.

I took her advice.

I felt one hundred percent better when I woke up. Well, actually, maybe seventy-five percent better, but it was still a big improvement. I ate some crackers, and that helped, too.

I called over to Lauren's to see how she was doing. She said she was just getting up, but that I should come over.

Just before I left, the phone rang. I hesitated for three rings, and really thought about not answering. But for some reason, I thought of what Callie might say about avoiding Mom, so I picked up the phone to try to do the right thing. But it wasn't Mom.

"It's about time," Hal said. "It was ringing forever."

"Sorry. I was doing something." I wondered how to get off the phone.

"Listen, I'm going to make this quick, because your mother's in the shower and she doesn't know I'm calling you. I wanted to let you know that every time she gets off the phone with you, she's upset. And I don't like it."

I don't really give a rat's ass *what* you like, I thought. But I was good. I kept my mouth shut and he went on.

"So here's the deal, champ. Things are going to be different. Your Mom gave you way too much room to do what you want, is my opinion. So we're going to run a much tighter ship from now on. You do not run this show, and the sooner you understand that, the sooner we can get this ball game back in play. What do you have to say to that?"

I say fuck you, Hal. "Well, you mixed a few metaphors, there."

"This is what I'm talking about. You better find a way to lose that wise-ass attitude or you're going to be in a world of shit, believe you me. The shower just went off, so I'm going to hang up now. Remember what I said, chief. Be smart."

He hung up without saying good-bye. I felt like the innocent guy in the movie who gets threatened by the gangster. Usually the innocent guy ends up wiping out all the bad guys in the end, in a big blaze of gunfire. As comforting as that idea was, this wasn't a movie and I wasn't at all sure that there would be a happy ending.

Lauren's brother was a gawky ninth-grader with a face that looked like a bad version of Lauren. Everything was too big. It was like looking at Lauren in a carnival mirror.

He sat in the living room, with his leg hanging over the arm of the couch as he watched MTV and ate Cheez Doodles. As far as I could tell, the kid didn't have vocal cords.

Lauren took me into the kitchen and stuck some Strawberry Pop-Tarts in the toaster oven.

"So when is the party at Donna's?" she asked. "Ten?"

"I don't know. I told you I can't go."

"Very funny."

"What?"

"You're kidding."

"I'm not kidding. I told you."

"Well, I thought you were joking around. It's New Year's Eve. What are you doing?"

"I'm going over to Callie's."

"Wait a minute. What is this? Are you saying you want to spend New Year's with some practical stranger, your part-time reading job person, instead of with me?"

"She's not a stranger, for one. And two, I told you about this. She's really alone. You have all those people to hang out with."

"But I wanted to be with you most."

"Well I know, but this is something that's important."

"And I'm not?"

"You're important. Of course you're important. But this is a special situation."

She looked at me for a couple of seconds, shook her head, and turned her back to me, making herself busy at the toaster oven. I didn't know someone could get so deeply involved with preparing Pop-Tarts.

"You understand?" I asked.

"Do what you want," she said.

"Well, I'm just saying. Do you understand why I need to do this?"

"Do whatever you want to do."

She wouldn't turn to me.

And that made any guilt I might have felt turn to frustration. "You know something, Lauren. I just don't need this crap right now."

"Well me either."

"I have a lot on my mind."

"Good for you. You can talk about all of it with your great friend when you're with her on New Year's Eve."

"You know . . . " I said, not knowing at all what I meant to say.

"What?"

"Forget it," I said, and I left.

I got to Callie's at nine. We had agreed to spend New Year's together, since we both hated holidays and all. I had warned her not to cook anything heavy, that I had a bit of a touchy stomach.

We turned her TV on, picking *Rockin' New Year's Eve* because it was the most mockable. I described what was on the screen to her.

"So here's this boy group you've been hearing so much about. They're in matching white suits with sequins. They're all desperately trying to look tough by growing this scraggly facial hair."

"They sound like eunuchs."

"That's exactly how they look. Skinny eunuchs. Good call."

We did this all the way up to the countdown. Callie twisted the wire on the top of a bottle of champagne. "I'm serving alcohol to a minor. You won't turn me in?"

"Not this time." She held the bottle out to me. "You want to do it?" she asked.

"Okay," I said. I pushed up on the cork, easing it. It was actually kind of suspenseful.

"Watch your eyes," she said.

It popped and hit the ceiling near the corner of the room. I poured for us. The countdown started.

"I hate this part. How about if we turn it off and just ignore the actual moment?" she said.

"Fine with me." I turned off the TV. "So, how about those Jets?" I said.

"Lovely weather, don't you think?" she said.

"And how about those Jets?"

We exchanged clichés for about two minutes. I looked at my watch.

"It's done," I said.

"Good. Cheers." She raised her glass and drank.

"Here's looking at you, kid," I said. I didn't like the champagne at all.

I gave her a hug. She kissed my cheek.

We put the TV back on and sat for a while.

"Another year," Callie said.

"It seems to keep happening."

"Hm." She thought for a minute. "I'm going to ask you

to do something that may make you feel a little strange."

"Everything makes me feel a little strange."

"Well, this is kind of different."

"What?"

"Tell me what I look like?"

"What do you mean?"

"I mean, I haven't seen myself in ten years. I don't really know what I look like."

The thought was almost inconceivable to me. Not that it was a great big thrill, but I could look in the mirror any time I wanted. For good or bad, I knew what I looked like. It just never occurred to me, since we all take it for granted, but Callie had no idea what she looked like anymore.

"Would you?" she asked.

"Of course. I don't know where to begin."

She moved closer to me and faced me. "Just tell me what you see."

"Well, you're very pretty."

"That doesn't help. I need specifics. Pretty doesn't mean anything to me."

"Okay. Your hair is kind of light orange. Strawberry blond, I think it's called?"

"Go on."

"Well, you have a small nose. There's a little bump on the bridge. You have light freckles over your nose, very light. You have a pretty mouth, oh, sorry. It's small, kind of, and your lips are sort of a deep pink. You wouldn't need to wear lipstick. You're petite, I guess. I don't know what else to say."

She smiled. "You skipped one thing. My eyes."

"Okay. Your eyes. Well, um. There are very fine pale scars around them. Your eyes are . . . They're bright green, and clear. I know this may not mean anything to you, but it's the best way to say it. They're very striking. Kind of magnetic. They look . . . They look true. I don't know."

"That's very good. One last thing. How old do I look?"

"I don't know. I'm a bad judge."

"Twenty-eight?"

"I don't know."

"Older?"

"I can't tell."

"I have this feeling I look a little older."

"I just don't know."

"Tell the truth."

"I can't."

I couldn't tell her the truth, even though I really knew at that point.

The truth was that I was in love with her.

in the dark

I had a hard time sleeping that night. There was too much going on in my head. Trying to collect my thoughts was like playing tag with a bunch of ten-year-olds on Rollerblades, in the dark. The ideas came whipping around and before I could grab onto one, it was already gone. I got up and fiddled with the answering machine. I don't know exactly what I did, but I got it working again.

I slept until two-thirty. I felt kind of crappy when I got up, just overtired and stiff. I had a bowl of Honeycombs and took a long shower. The machine was blinking with one message when I got out. I hit the play button.

Mom's voice sounded cheerful. "Hi, kid. Just wanted to call to say 'Happy New Year.' I know you don't believe it, but I really think it will be a happy year for us. Talk to you later."

Yeah, right. It was off to a great start. I had to try to make up with Lauren somehow. I'd left things in a pretty bad way with her and I wasn't happy about it. I didn't know what to do about her, but I couldn't just leave it. I dialed her number.

"Hi," she said in not the friendliest voice.

"How was the party?"

"Fine."

"Who was there?"

"I don't know. Kids."

"What's the matter?"

"Nothing."

Yeah, right. "It's about last night. About me not going with you."

There was no answer.

"I'm sorry."

Again, no answer.

"Lauren, I'm sorry. It was something I really needed to do."

"Well, I'm pissed. What can I tell you?"

I was starting to get annoyed. She was not exactly being understanding. "I don't know. There isn't much more I can say, except that I'm sorry."

We batted this around for a while. Finally, she said, "Okay, well. I'll get over it, I'm sure. What are you doing?"

"Nothing. Why don't we get together?"

"Everyone's over here and they're watching football. You want to come over? Watch the game with my brother and stepfather?"

"Not really," I said. Watching traffic would have had more appeal to me.

"Should I come over there?"

"Sounds good," I said.

We watched TV for a while. I made some mac and cheese.

"Is this what you cooked for her?" she asked.

I gave her a look.

"I was just kidding," she said. "Lighten up."

She may have been partly kidding, but she was also partly serious.

After a while, we started fooling around. It was okay, but I had a nagging guilty feeling, since I realized that I was pretty much in love with Callie. I wasn't totally into it with Lauren.

"What's the matter?" she said.

"Nothing. Come on," I said.

She kissed me harder, went after my ears with her teeth. My ears are kind of sensitive. I started to think about Callie. It's kind of creepy, I guess, but I sort of pictured myself with Callie a little bit. What I'm trying to say is that I basically pretended that Lauren was Callie.

And I instantly got turned on.

But when I touched her, I knew she wasn't. She wasn't ready, not at all. Which was the total opposite of how she had been every other time.

Now I didn't know if girls have control of that particular bodily function, but I had the feeling that she was doing it deliberately to send some kind of message to me.

"What's the matter? You're not . . . you know," I said. I didn't know the polite way to put it.

"I don't know. I guess I'm not really in the mood for this. Sorry."

Wait, we're stopping now? I wanted to ask. Is that allowed?

She rolled away from me and crossed her arms, turning to the TV, which was still on. I was pretty sure that this was some kind of mind game Lauren was playing. She wanted me to fall all over myself apologizing again, beg her forgiveness, and plead for her love. Or sex, anyhow.

Well, I wouldn't do it. I did the right thing, going to be with Callie. Lauren was obviously too emotionally immature to handle it. She was just really needy, and I was starting to get sick of it. And this whole game she was playing was kind of making me mad. Another sign of being emotionally immature. She was the total opposite of Callie.

I wasn't going to apologize again or beg her for anything. Screw that.

We lay there in silence, each of us alone with our thoughts.

Going back to school was pretty awful. As if I didn't have enough on my mind, I had to be a good little schoolboy. I was prepared to tell Mr. Horwich that my mother got called away on a business trip, but he never called me to the office. He must have forgotten that he told me not to come back after vacation without her. Somehow, I got a slide on that, as Glenn would say.

But I didn't get a slide with Mr. Brody. He pulled me aside after class.

"I don't know what happened to you, Kirk. It's like

you're bottoming out. You're a bright kid, but you sit there like a dummy, no offense. From my point of view, it looks like you just gave up. You don't care. Is there something wrong?"

"Everything's fine."

"Is there something I can do to help you?"

He looked at me and I had to look away. He was a decent guy, but I couldn't let him get involved.

"I'm fine. Thanks for asking."

I started to go, but he stopped me. "Kirk? You know, you have choices. You could go to a really good college and meet lots of interesting people. Or you could end up bagging groceries in the supermarket. You just have to decide."

"Just decide. It's that easy?"

"I didn't say it was easy. I'm saying you have to make a decision about what it is you really want. And then you have to work to make it all happen."

I had to do something that was going to suck, big time. I waited on Lauren's front step, waiting for her to answer the door so I could break up with her. I didn't know exactly when or how or, I guess even if, I was going to be with Callie. That was all to come. But I felt like a real bastard even trying to go on with Lauren while I felt the way I did about Callie.

Traitor, she gave you a chance, you cut her off
Trade her, the girl for the woman

Youth and age
Euthanasia
Put the dying relationship out of your misery
Put it out of your mind;
                    Don't go
    out of your mind.

"Hi," she said. "Come on in."

"I can't stay. I just wanted to talk to you for a minute."

"What's wrong?"

"Lauren, you know I really like you." She nodded and kind of tightened her mouth. I guess she saw where this was headed. I was so cold, my back hurt from clenching against the shivering.

"The thing is, I just think we shouldn't see too much of each other," I said.

"We're breaking up," she said. "Okay, fine."

"Fine?"

"What do you want me to say? You think I'm going to beg you? I've never begged a guy in my life and I'm not about to start now. Not for you."

"I thought we could still be friends," I said.

"Why?"

"Why?" I repeated, feeling like a moronic parrot.

"That never works. When it's over, it's over. Forget about it."

Wow. Pretty harsh. Fine, then.

"Sorry."

She shrugged again. I turned around and started walking away.

"I was wrong about you," she said. "I thought you were different."

I felt like total crap as I kept walking.

I couldn't keep Callie out of my mind at all. Not even for five minutes. It was a really weird feeling, being in love. It was almost like this constant feeling of something being missing, of longing. It felt like part of me wasn't there when I wasn't with her. I couldn't stop thinking about her. It must be what it feels like to be addicted to something.

But there was also this total, complete excitement and, like, pure happiness. She was alive on this earth. Her existence was enough to make me feel sort of exhilarated. For the past few days, looking forward to being with her, talking to her, seeing her, just gave me this amazing feeling.

There was something I had been wanting to do for a while and I had to pick up some stuff from the drugstore to do it. On Thursday, I wasn't reading to Callie and Glenn was deep in rehearsal with the Socks. I stopped at the drugstore on the way home from school.

As soon as I got home, I went into the bathroom and took out my stuff. I checked my watch before I started. I cut pieces of gauze into egg-sized ovals and I tore off strips of adhesive tape. As soon as it was four o'clock, I covered both my eyes with the gauze and tape. I made it so there was just a tiny hint of light filtering through.

I wanted to go eight hours and try to get a sense of what it felt like for Callie.

I put my hands out and used them to guide me. I walked down the hall to my room, my hands in front of me. I was nervous. It felt like I was going to miss something and bang my face against a door.

For a while I just tried moving from room to room. Then I went down the stairs, feeling ahead with my toes, like I was checking the water in a swimming pool. It was nerve-racking, but a little exciting. I didn't plan to leave the house, because I would probably have gotten run over or something. That was okay, I had plenty to explore at home.

I ran into trouble when I went into the refrigerator. I couldn't tell what anything was. Suddenly, I understood very clearly why Callie was so careful about where things were placed in her kitchen. I felt around and tried to guess, but then I ended up opening jars and bottles. I couldn't tell one can of soda from another, though. I knocked a quart of milk over and I could hear the milk chugging out of the container. I got it upright and felt my way to the sink and got a sponge. It was hard to tell if I had gotten all the milk up. It might be all over the inside of the refrigerator. If I didn't get all of it, it would go sour and smell. I thought about lifting the eye patches for just a second, just to clean up. But Callie didn't have that choice, and I don't know, it felt like kind of a betrayal of her if I did it. I cleaned up the best I could.

I put the TV on for a while and found that it wasn't too hard to figure out what was going on for most shows. But some things, like cartoons that didn't have a lot of dialogue, were pretty hard to follow. And for other shows, I wondered what people looked like.

After a while, I started to feel kind of edgy. I didn't know what time it was or how long I had been doing it. I put on the news and waited for them to mention the time. I had only been doing it for an hour and a half.

As the night went on, I went back and forth between pretty much two emotions: depression and anxiety. I would get this deep sad feeling. It was just this feeling of being so cut off. It felt very lonely.

I also kept feeling like I was going to panic. It was this bad feeling that started in my chest and stomach. My heart would start beating hard and I was really nervous all of a sudden and I just wanted to pull off the patches. But I wouldn't let myself do it. Of course, I realized that there was a huge difference between my little game and Callie's blindness.

I went to the phone and dialed. That was one thing I could do okay.

"Hello?" Callie said.

"Hi, it's Kirk."

"How are you? I'm in the middle of cooking."

"Oh. Okay. I won't bother you."

"You're not bothering me. What's wrong? You sound kind of off."

"Nothing. I was just . . . I was thinking about you and I wanted to give you a call. Just to hear your voice."

"Oh, wow. That's really nice. Let me call you back?"

"It's okay . . . I'll see you, talk to you tomorrow."

"You sure?"

"Yeah. I have stuff to do, anyway."

"Okay. See you tomorrow," she said.

"See you then." I put the phone down. I didn't want to tell her what I was doing. It was possible she would see it as kind of stupid, or childish, or maybe even insulting in a way, like I was making a game of her life. But that wasn't what I was doing. It was just for me. It was a way I felt I could understand Callie just a tiny bit better, to feel closer to her.

I stuck it out until midnight. And for a while, the light blinded me worse than the darkness.

At school on Friday, I saw Lauren in the hallway, hanging around with Glenn's friends. Our eyes met.

She gave the harshest look anybody ever gave me in my life.

I was pretty sure that she hated me.

I looked down and walked on by.

I felt a hand on my shoulder. I turned. It was Glenn. "You okay, Hob?" he asked.

"I'm great."

"Hey, what can I say, man? Love hurts. But before you know it, you'll find someone else and start the whole messed-up deal all over again."

I smiled. If he only knew.

We finished the book on loneliness. It was great writing, but I couldn't really relate to it at that point, not feeling like I did. After we finished, we went into the kitchen. She had some kind of curry thing going.

"You know, I've noticed. You really like making stews and soups. You don't like to bake or anything like that?"

"There are some things I can't do as well. Things in a mix work best for me. But some things are a lot easier to cook when you can see."

"Well, what if I helped? I can see pretty well."

"So I've noticed. Maybe we'll try it." She smiled at me and touched my elbow. She moved her hand up my arm and patted me on the shoulder. "Have a seat."

The way she touched me was really very affectionate. As I played back so many of the things she said to me, the things she did for me, the way she was with me, it was becoming pretty clear to me that I wasn't the only one with certain strong feelings. Yes, I definitely could see very well.

Then she leaned over to put the food in my bowl. Now I really couldn't help it. Her shirt was kind of open a little and it was right in front of me, and I just couldn't help but kind of look. All I'll say is she wasn't wearing anything underneath. I know how creepy it sounds, me looking down her shirt and all. But it's not so bad if you think that she might have been doing it, bending over like that in front of me, on purpose.

Things were becoming very clear to me.

Friday came. The big night. I was dressed in jeans and a black T-shirt.

I drove to Callie's to pick her up. I wasn't in that much

of a rush. I left plenty of time, so we could talk before we went to the club.

She opened the door for me. She looked great. She had on a deep dark green shirt.

"I don't remember the last time I've been to a club. I'll probably be the oldest one there."

"I doubt it."

She laughed. Boy, I loved that laugh.

"I'm really glad you wanted to come to this," I said. "I think it's going to be a really special night."

"Me, too."

My heart was pounding. All the clocks ticked, marking time.

"There's something I wanted to tell you about," I said.

"It sounds kind of important."

"It is." I was afraid I would start gulping air, or panting.

"Another big secret to reveal?"

"Well, huh. Huh." I was starting to sound like a mental patient. I tried to convince myself to stay cool, go with the flow, be the moonlight on the running water.

"Well, okay. I'm ready. Let's hear it."

I couldn't swallow.

"Callie?" I put my hands on her arms.

"What's up?"

"I really . . . love you," I said.

"Kirk," she said, so softly I almost couldn't hear it.

I took her in my arms and kissed her. It was soft and it felt like electricity. After a moment, she pulled back a bit and tilted her head down.

"Uh . . ." She was overwhelmed. Just like me.

She backed up and sat on the couch.

"I know it's been kind of awkward, trying to get the courage to admit these feelings. It might have been the age thing, or maybe the whole idea of our relationship starting with me basically working for you. But we're so past that stuff. It's going to take a little bit of courage for us to get over that hesitation, but once we do, we'll never have to turn back."

She took a long breath. "Kirk. You have a girlfriend."

"Oh, I broke up with her. That wasn't real. This is."

She didn't say anything.

"So, what I was thinking is that, now that we've gotten everything out in the open, I could really just move in. That way we can really be together. Like we should be."

"Oh my God," she said softly.

"I know. Isn't it great for it to be out in the open? Don't you feel great?"

"No." And she didn't look great. I went and sat next to her. I took hold of her hands.

"I understand. It's kind of scary. A lot all at once."

She pulled her hands away.

"You're very . . . confused. Honey, you really . . . You have this all wrong."

"No. I think I have it all right."

"Listen to me. I'm telling you. I'm sorry, but you're wrong."

I looked at her. "Are you telling me that you don't love me, too?"

"Kirk. I love you. Really. But not that way."

Not that way.

Three words, three syllables.

"Well, I refuse to believe that," I said. "You're fighting it. But underneath, I know how you really feel. If you could see the way you . . . the way you look at me . . . "

"But I can't, goddammit, Kirk! I can't 'see' the way I look at you. I can't see and I can't look at you. I am blind, or hadn't you noticed?"

"You are not. You see better than anyone I know!"

"Oh for God's sake, Kirk. Stop it. You can't make things be what they're not, just because you want it. That's kid stuff. You have to grow up."

"I don't even know what you're talking about."

"Yes you do. You're smart. I'm saying that, yes, I love you. I love you like a brother, I love you like a friend. Like one of the best friends I ever had. But I don't love you like a lover. I'm saying I'm sorry to hurt you, but there will never be a romance between us. It's not ever going to happen."

There was a long silence. I felt like I had a golf ball stuck in my throat. I had to get out of there. I tried to come up with some kind of exit line, something smart, or witty, or bittersweet, something that would give me a way out with some tiny shred of self-esteem intact.

But there was no line. It wasn't a movie. There was nothing good to say.

"I have to go," I said.

"Kirk."

But I didn't wait. I pulled the door shut behind me. The porch light was out. I stepped into the dark.

broken

I believe that there is such a thing as a born loser. The person who always seems to get into messed-up situations, or manages to make a normal situation messed-up. This is a person who bad luck seems to follow. Vacations with rain every day. Things always drop, plates keep falling and breaking. The train just left. Oh, sorry we just sold the last one: if you had only been here five minutes ago. Wow, I've been cutting hair for ten years and this never happened before. Hm, I thought these things were factory-tested and weren't supposed to break.

I love you, but not that way. What the hell were you thinking? Are you a moron? How in the hell could you think I would have feelings for you? Who exactly do you think you are? Somebody?

Hell, a blind person could see you're a loser.

I decided to stop home before going to Glenn's show. To be honest, I kept getting the feeling that I was going to cry.

I kept swallowing and opening my eyes wide, thinking that it might keep the tears from filling my eyes.

I walked in and shut the front door.

"Surprise!"

I shouted, my heart seized.

Surprise was right. Sitting on the couch was Mom.

"Oh my God," I said. "I didn't . . . "

Could this night get any worse? Actually it could. And did. I heard a toilet flush and Hal came into the living room. "Hey, champ," he said.

"What are you doing here?" I said.

"Well, we had to come back to take care of business, right?" Mom said.

"What?"

"Put our houses on the market, pack up," Hal said.

"And get you," Mom said.

Get me. God.

"Here we are, all together," Mom said. She actually smiled and she got up to give me a hug. I felt like I was going to choke.

Hal strolled over to us. "What's with the black outfit? You going to a funeral?" I swear, he had a smirk on his face that made me want to smash him in the mouth.

"I have to go," I said.

"Go? We just got here. We have a lot to talk about."

"I can't. I really have to go."

"Where?" Hal asked, his tone a little tougher than I could handle right then.

"Somewhere."

"Well, we need to talk," Mom said.

"I told you, I can't."

"Hey," Hal said sharply. "Remember what we talked about?"

I reached for the door and opened it. It felt like my heart was beating out of rhythm and I couldn't get my breathing right. I felt a hard ache in my throat and my eyes were welling up. I'd be damned if I would let Hal see me cry. I had to get out of there, quickly, or I was going to lose it.

"Kirk?"

"I have to go," I said, but it probably came out as a whisper. I couldn't really speak.

I moved to go out the door and that's when Hal grabbed my arm. No adult ever grabbed me like that.

"You're not going anywhere," he said.

I tried to pull away, but his fingers dug into my bicep and gripped me. "Let go of me!" I tugged, but he was strong, a lot stronger than me. He reached for my other arm or maybe my neck, and I ducked and dove out of the way.

I twisted free and ran out the door.

They shouted something at me as I ran away, but I couldn't hear them. I couldn't hear anything.

It was raining as I drove to the bar. The whole way over, I worked hard to control my breathing and to resist the urge to gun the engine and roar down the road.

The bouncer took a quick look at the fake ID Glenn had gotten for me, shrugged, and waved me in. The place was a pit. It was dark, filled with smoke and sweaty people in flannel shirts and leather jackets. A bunch of people wearing sunglasses and tank tops, with arms thicker than my legs, were playing pool. There were a bunch of kids, obviously teenagers with fake IDs, around the little stage area. Glenn and the Socks were finishing their set-up. I saw what Glenn meant about the lead singer: he was wearing some kind of tights or something, an enormous halo of hair, and was communing with a candle he had set up on one of the amplifiers.

Glenn caught my eye and gave me a smile. He stepped up to the microphone, flicked it on, and tapped it.

"Sound check. Midget. Midget. Midget."

Very funny. I was in a real joking mood.

Donna found me and gave me a hug. "This is so exciting," she said.

"Absolutely," I said. She handed me a beer. I chugged it. I had two more before the leader of the Socks stepped up to the microphone. "Uh, one, two . . . "

My eardrums almost imploded when the Socks hit their first chords.

I went over to the bar and ordered another beer. In preparation, I hadn't shaved for almost a week and had some stubble on my chin and upper lip. The bartender looked at me and gave me the beer.

I turned back to look at the stage, and that's when I saw Lauren at the bar, practically next to me. Though she was friends with Glenn before I was, somehow it didn't occur to me that she'd be there. I also didn't expect to see her there with her arm around some other guy. He was someone I'd seen around school, something Graham.

Lauren turned to me.

"What," she said, loudly to be heard above the music. "What are you looking at?"

I must have been staring. "Sure didn't take you long," I said.

"What, did you think I would become a nun after we broke up?"

"Not too likely."

She shook her head, took the guy's arm and moved away, a little closer to the stage.

I watched Lauren and that guy. It's not that I was jealous, not really. I just couldn't believe that she'd been with me just a few days before and there she was with another guy so fast. Obviously I didn't mean anything to her after all.

I finished up the rest of my beer and moved closer to Lauren and the guy.

"Hey," I said. "You have a lot of girlfriends before?" I asked him.

"Kirk, go away," Lauren said. I didn't really feel like being dismissed.

"Seriously. I'm just asking. Things work out okay for you? Stuff going right for you in your life? And now you have this great girlfriend."

"Why don't you get lost, kid."

"I am lost."

The Socks finished their song and Glenn stepped up to the microphone. "Here's one you probably haven't heard yet." He started playing one of the songs we wrote. There was a little soft backup from the band, but when Glenn started to sing, for some reason, I couldn't understand the words. There was some kind of distortion. My words were totally lost.

"I wrote that. I wrote the words," I said.

"I'm real impressed," the Graham guy said. I looked at him. He was pretty good-looking, pretty tall, probably athletic. Confident. He was everything I'm not.

"You really think this is going to work?" I asked him. "You're going to make a total ass of yourself. You think you're something special, but you're not. You're nothing. You're a tree and you're stiff and you're going to get blown away."

He stood up off the bar stool. "Are you threatening me? I'll kill you with one punch."

"You're so strong, right? You think you have control, but like the lady said, control is an illusion. Let me tell you something. Your whole world is about to turn to shit and there's not a damn thing you can do about it."

"You're looking to get hurt," he said.

"Loser. Loser. I'd really like to see you try. I'd like to see you fucking try to hurt me!"

I guess I kind of shoved him in the chest. He shoved me backward and I crashed into someone behind me, who spilled a drink and pushed me back at the kid.

I took a wild swing at Graham, and I hit him on the side of the head. He punched me in the eye, which knocked me backward.

"Back off, or I'm gonna hurt you."

There was no way I could stop. I just couldn't back away. I dove at him, swinging my fists at him.

So he pounded me. It was pretty clear that I was no

match for this guy. He was popping me in the face, but I wouldn't stop. I kept going back at him. I was kind of growling or shouting and I couldn't stop swinging at him.

He hit me in the stomach and I gasped in. I couldn't breathe, but I still dove at him again.

There was a high-pitched squeal of feedback. A second later, an arm came from behind me, over my shoulder, and wrapped across my chest. I was pulled backward, up off my feet. Graham came at me and I kicked out at him. I must have hit him, because he made a sound and charged at me.

He hit me pretty hard, square in the nose and I heard—or felt—something like a pop and warm wet blood rushed over my mouth and chin. My eyes flooded and I felt dizzy.

But I was off my feet, carried out.

I was shoved out into the parking lot. I turned around and took a wild, roundhouse swing.

Glenn stepped out of the way and wrestled me to the ground. I was still fighting back.

"It's me," he said into my ear. "Stop, it's me."

He got me so I couldn't move at all. I felt my jeans soaking up rain from the wet asphalt. "Let go of me."

"Relax," he said. "Relax."

I went slack. He slowly let go of me and lifted me to my feet.

I was dizzy and dazed, staggering in circles. It sounded like a prison riot inside the bar. The band started playing again, minus the lead guitar.

"What was *that*?" he said.

"I don't know."

He grabbed a handful of snow from a big drift on the edge of the parking lot. "Here. Put this on your face." He put the snow in my hand and pressed it against my nose. It burned.

"Gimme your car keys," he said.

"Why?"

"Now." I handed them over. "You're not driving. I'm going back in to finish the set and then we'll go. My car's open. Just lay down in the back and wait for me," Glenn told me.

"I'm fine."

"Yeah? Don't look in the mirror."

"It would have to be an improvement."

"Well, that's true. Do me a favor. Try not to bleed too much on the seat."

"Yeah, we wouldn't want to mess up the car, right? I'll try to coagulate a little faster."

"Excellent."

"That was a relaxing little evening. Thanks for inviting me."

"Anytime. So just wait for me. I'll be back in a little while."

There was a rush of sound from the bar when he opened the door. I caught a glimpse of Donna looking out for me before she and Glenn disappeared back into the bar.

I looked at the snow I'd had against my face. The streaks of frozen blood looked purple, almost black under the parking lot lights. I threw the bloody ice away.

I didn't want to wait in his car. I just wanted to get away. I didn't know where I was going, but I started walking.

It began to rain harder. I ducked my head and hunched my shoulders and kept walking nowhere.

The rain came heavier, but there was no cover. I kept walking and relaxed my shoulders, stood up straighter. The water started to loosen the blood coating my face, to wash it away.

The rain didn't bother me anymore. Someone had told me, you can't fight a rainstorm.

blind sighted

"Please don't hang up," I said.

"I wouldn't do that to you," Callie said.

"Were you sleeping?"

"No. I'm up."

"There's so much I want to clear up."

"Me too."

"When can I see you?"

"As soon as you'd like."

"Is now too soon?"

Of course, she didn't react to how my face looked. She couldn't see me. As usual, with her, I totally forgot how I looked.

"Listen, all kinds of stuff has happened. A lot. My mother came back. Um. I got in a fight at Glenn's show.

"Are you okay?"

"I'm all right, but a little banged up. There's so much in my head. I swear I'm not running, but I need a little time to work some of it out. I won't blame you if you say no, especially after last night, but is there any chance I could stay here for a day or two?"

She reached out and put her hand on my arm. "Of course. Whatever you need."

I called Mom and told her where I was. "I'm sorry about before. And I'm okay, but I just need a little time. I'm safe here."

"You don't want to come home?"

"Not yet. I really need this time."

"Okay. Call me."

I got upstairs and went into the bathroom. I turned on the light, looking down into the sink. Okay, let's have a look at it, Skip. I looked up into the mirror.

Mistake.

The bridge of my nose was hugely swollen and the color of a plum. There was dried blood caking my nostrils and upper lip. My lips looked like they had been injected with grape juice. I had a dark red bruise on the outside of my right eye. The weirdest looking part was the bright red spot on the white part of my eye, like from some kind of burst vessel. I pulled my T-shirt over my head and when I lifted my arms up, it felt like getting stabbed in the side. There was a rosy bruise on my ribs, coincidentally fist-sized.

I washed up as best as I could and took four aspirin. I

went to bed in Callie's spare bedroom. I didn't want to think about anything. I just wanted to get some sleep. Say for about five years.

I woke up at three in the afternoon. I went to the bathroom and had a look. It was even worse than before. It was an ugly dark, dark purple on the bridge of my nose and on the sides, under my eyes. It hurt to touch. I figured maybe it was broken. The blood spot took over the whole white part of half my eye. It was really freaky-looking, like I was an alien or something. The bruise on my ribs was much darker, and it hurt there when I breathed in deep. I guessed maybe I had a broken rib or two.

I drank water from the sink and went back to bed.

But I couldn't sleep anymore. I had so much to work out.

I don't know what it was, but it was like I had gotten all the idiocy beaten out of me. It was like thinking back about all the things you believed when you were a little kid. Step on a crack, break whatever. There is a tooth fairy. Life is fair. Love is blind. And then you grow up a little and you go, How could I possibly have thought all that? Now you can see everything clearly. You lived in a fantasy world, but you've stepped through the door into the real world. It all looks different from this side.

I had to fix all the things I'd messed up. I wasn't happy with what I did to Lauren. I messed up Glenn's big night. I had to work things out with Mom. And the most important thing I had to do was find a way to fix things with

Callie. I was pretty much horrified at what I had said to her, what I had done. I couldn't imagine what the hell I was thinking.

I sat down and started to write.

I was at Callie's for two days. Of course, she made sure I ate. She somehow could see that I wasn't ready to talk. We went about forty hours and barely spoke at all. And the amazing thing was that I didn't feel alone. Even without speaking, we understood each other.

I called Mom each day. She was worried and confused, but she trusted me that I was okay. I spent the days writing the whole thing out, thinking and writing. I felt like I could see things clearly. I had some ideas. On Monday, I waited until five and I called Lauren. Her stepfather answered.

"Hi, Mr. Mason. It's Kurt."

"Who?"

"Kurt? Lauren's . . . friend?"

"I thought your name was Kirk."

"Oh. I guess you're right."

"You don't even know who you are, son?"

"Well, sir. You know, sometimes I get a little confused."

"Don't we all, son. Hold on."

I held on for a while. "Hello?"

"Lauren? How are you?"

"I'm okay. How about you?"

"I'm fine."

"That was some show," she said.

"Yeah. Listen, I'd like to see you. Can you meet me? Outside? Now?"

"Um. Okay."

"I have to warn you. I don't exactly look great."

"I don't care."

I waited on the corner of her block. It was cold, but it felt good. It helped me feel clear.

"Oh my God," Lauren said when she saw my face.

"It looks worse than it feels."

"It looks pretty bad."

"Lauren. Look. I don't know what to say. I think I was pretty rotten about how I handled everything with you. And then the whole thing with your boyfriend. That was ridiculous and totally out of line. I'm sorry. I swear, I didn't mean for anyone to get hurt."

"You know what? People get hurt in relationships. Part of the game. You don't wanna get hurt, don't play."

"True."

"Hey, I was just trying to have some fun."

"But was I *totally* wrong? We did have something pretty good for a while."

"Yeah, for a while. But it was never going to last. You're kind of intense, and so am I. Too much stuff going on. I don't need that kind of grief."

I nodded. "Two too intense."

"You can't have two that are the same. It doesn't work. Too much of one thing. You need a better mix."

"Better balance."

"You got it."

I stopped at Glenn's.

"The midget warrior," he said.

"Look. I wanted to say I'm sorry for messing up your show."

"Our show. And don't worry about it. They say it ain't a party till something gets broke. Too bad it had to be you."

"I guess it did add a whole element of performance art. Still, I'm sorry I ruined it."

"You didn't. And our stuff went over pretty good. We need to work on some of the lyrics, though. And I have some more ideas. If you're up for it."

"Definitely."

He slapped my back as I walked toward the street.

"Hey. I think we're playing there again next week. Wanna come?"

"Can't wait."

Callie sat in her chair. I paced. "I want to go back and erase the other night. I want us to forget everything I said."

"Well, you know we really can't forget it."

"Well, then, can we call it a bunch of crazy talk that doesn't count?"

"Kirk. Look. It's important that you told me how you feel. I felt really horrible about the whole thing, but it did happen."

"I know. I know, and I can't tell you how bad I feel about

what I did to you. What I put you through. There aren't words for how I feel. Horrible. Miserifying. I don't know."

"I think I understand. You know, I've been trying to think of what I did that might have misled you."

"It wasn't anything you did. It was me. Callie, I was just acting like a little kid. It was just like a really immature, you know, interpretation of my feelings. I mean, I do love you. I really, really do. But I understand that just because it's this totally intense feeling, it doesn't mean that it's, it's romance, for lack of a better word. I mean, what it is, is I'm not used to having such really strong, strong feelings and I got a little confused."

She nodded. "Believe me. I understand."

"There's something I wanted to read to you."

"I'm all ears."

Moonlight on the water
What her ideas mean to me
I was blind to what she offered
Meanings misconstrued, imbued
I saw what I wanted to see.
She moved me how she moved,
with no vision to ruin her sight.
Balance is her strongest suit
She knows how not to fall
Into feelings that destroy her view.

She sees the trees, the way they sway
She sees the wind, she knows the way
To see inside my mind.

My vision was twenty-twenty
She showed me the illusions
Confusing me, me refusing
To see.

Her eyes are bad, she cannot see
But she can read between the lines
I'm learning to see the invisible
I'm learning to live
She's teaching me to see
To be
Blind sighted

I looked up, into Callie's eyes. "I know it's not perfect. It's a work in progress. Kinda like me."

She smiled. I felt a dull ache start in my throat. I tried to swallow, but couldn't. I made a little coughing sound, trying to make sure my voice was still there before starting to speak.

"Do you think there's any way we could just try to go back to the way things were before? Because, if you ask me, the way we were before? It was the best. I want it back."

"I can do it if you can."

"I can. I want to."

"Me too."

She got up and put out her hand. I took it and we hugged. I held on for life.

"I'm so sorry, Callie. I'm sorry for everything."

"Don't be. Remember the moonlight on the moving

water. We're still here. We go with the flow. 'Sorry' is a waste. Life's too short."

She couldn't see me cry. But she could feel it. And she cried, too.

We stayed up all night, talking and eating. I won't say it was like nothing ever happened. All the stuff that happened, all that was said, it still existed. But it was in the past. You can't undo a bruise or a break. But it can heal. And sometimes, I guess, something that was broken heals even stronger.

It was dawn when I came to my latest idea.

Sometimes, once in a while, I come up with a good idea.

I had Mom and Hal come over to Callie's. I was very calm. I felt relaxed. I wasn't going to fight, I wasn't going to be rigid. I was going to bend. I was trying to flow.

"Here's my idea. I finish out the school year here. I've been slacking off and I don't want to leave it like that. I can straighten out in school. And I have friends that I'm not ready to leave yet."

Mom opened her mouth to speak.

"Wait, just let me finish. I'm not saying never, I'm just saying not yet. I finish the year. I stay here with Callie."

"Hold on. I'm not asking Callie to take care of you."

"It isn't like that," Callie said. "We take care of each other, really."

"We're a really good team and it would work out great.

So you guys can go out and get the restaurant started and not have to worry about me. You need money for the restaurant, or for a place out there, no problem. You can sell our house, because I'm here with Callie. See, this way, everybody wins."

Mom and Hal looked at each other.

"And what happens at the end of the school year?" Hal asked.

"I don't know. I'm not thinking that far ahead. We can see where things are then. One step at a time."

They didn't say anything.

"Mom? I think if you really look at it, you'll see. It's pretty clear."

Of course, Callie made a fantastic meal. We talked long into the night, working out details. Mom got to see what Callie was like. She got to see a little part of my new life, of the life I had made.

Mom looked at me. She smiled. It might have been a little bit of a sad smile, but I could see what it meant. We talked lots more over the next days and weeks, but at that moment when Mom looked at me, I knew then that it would work out.

I have a life here. I want to work to make it even better. I'm going to stay, at least for now. I'm not going to worry or try to control the future. I'm going to see things the way Callie sees them.

I never had a big sister, but if I did, I couldn't ask for a better one than Callie. We feel like family together.

It's funny that somebody recently asked me if I know who I am. That's the million dollar question.

There are some things I do know for sure. I'm not cool. I'm kind of strange. I'm pretty emotional. And I'm too damned small. And I'm okay with all that.

So, do I know who I am?

I guess maybe I don't know. Not yet.

But I'm getting there.